Back *to the*
Klondike

Yvonne Harris

Additional copies may be obtained directly from the publisher, prepaid. Send $9.95 plus $1.00 for postage and handling to:
    Tutshi Publishing
    7 Tutshi Road
    Whitehorse, Yukon
    Y1A 3R4

Canadian Cataloguing in Publication Data
Harris, Yvonne, (date)
    Back to the Klondike

    ISBN 0-9694977-5-X

    1. Klondike River Valley (Yukon)—Gold discoveries—Juvenile fiction. I. Title.
    PS8565.A6524B32 1999   jC813'.54   C99-910982-0
    PZ7.H244Ba 1999

Editorial Director: Nancy Foulds
Project Editor: Lee Craig
Production Manager: Jody Reekie
Layout & Production: Michelle Bynoe
Book Design: Michelle Bynoe
Cover Illustration: Catherine Deer
Cartography: Heather Markham (page 6), Ian Sheldon (page 7, 8)
Separations & Film: Elite Lithographers Company

CONTENTS

PREFACE

"Then one time, you know, when my father's mother was a little girl…there was a flood all over…It was because my father's people made fun of a seagull. And then a great flood came, and there was no place to be safe. That glacier broke that used to go across the Alsek. A great wave came along, and turned over the boats, and the young people were all flooded into the ocean."

The above story is how an Elder of the Tlingit Nation described the event that took place in the mid-1850s, as told to her by her mother. In *Back to the Klondike*, the ice dam breaks in 1898 and so begins Julianna's fictional adventure with the people who have occupied the Yukon and Alaska since time immemorial.

While the story of Julianna and Split the Waves is fiction, I have tried to accurately reflect the Tlingit and Southern Tutchone First Nation cultures and show the reader something of the amazing courage, strength and resilience of the native peoples. The oral history and research shows that the First Nation peoples travelled immense distances and could survive in the wilderness with nothing more than a few hand-made tools. Like Split the Waves, the young Tlingit man in this book, the First Nation peoples were great hunters, astute traders and clever entrepreneurs.

In the Tlingit culture, it is considered an insult to use another person's name. In respect of the Tlingit culture, no names are borrowed. With the exception of Split the Waves, the characters are named after animals, using the Tlingit translation of words as recorded by Aureal Krause one hundred years ago in his text, *The Tlingit Indians*.

Excellent Tlingit translations are being developed by the Aboriginal Language Services Branch of the Yukon government. However, the proper Tlingit translations, along with the diacritics, would be difficult to pronounce for most of the young people reading this book. As well, some Tlingit people are reluctant to share the translations with non-First Nations, if there is any commercial use of the translations.

DEDICATION

This book is dedicated to the people of Kwanlin Dun who took me into their hearts and their community. During my lifetime, a portion of the royalties from this book will go to Kwanlin Dun First Nation, to benefit their youth.

ACKNOWLEDGEMENTS

I want to thank the Elders of Kwanlin Dun who provided guidance and instruction to me, especially Ronald Bill, Violet Storer, Malcolm Dawson and Edwin Scurvey. I also want to acknowledge my rafting and kayaking companions, especially the group who travelled with me on the Tatshenshini and Alsek rivers.

I wish to acknowledge the assistance of the Burton House Society; the time I spent as writer-in-residence in Dawson City helped me better understand the Klondike era.

I am especially indebted to my son, Shane Kennedy, and his excellent staff at Lone Pine Publishing for their assistance with this book.

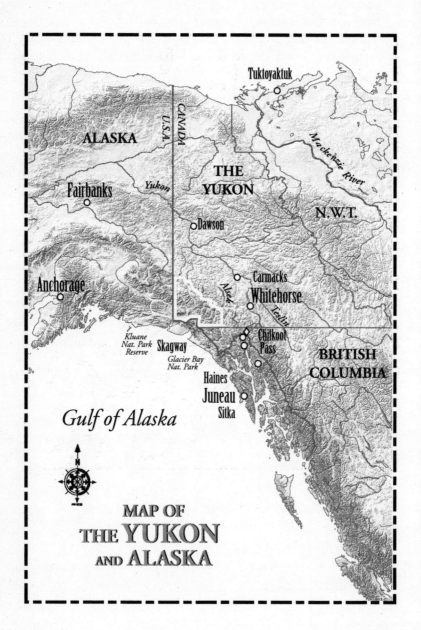

Tuktoyaktuk

ALASKA

CANADA
U.S.A.

Mackenzie River

Fairbanks

Yukon

THE
YUKON

N.W.T.

Dawson

Anchorage

Carmacks
Whitehorse

Alsek

Teslin

Kluane
Nat. Park
Reserve

Skagway

Chilkoot
Pass

Glacier Bay
Nat. Park

BRITISH
COLUMBIA

Haines
Juneau
Sitka

Gulf of Alaska

N

MAP OF
THE YUKON
AND ALASKA

From Turnback Canyon to the Longhouse of the Tagish

From Whitehorse to the Klondike

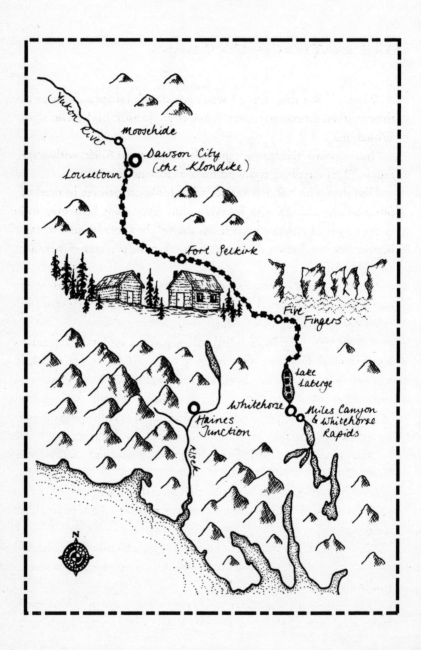

CHAPTER 1

THE OUTDOOR ED CLASS

"Marie, if you can't come I won't go either," Julianna declared as they walked home together from their junior high school in Whitehorse.

"But you love river trips, especially one like the Alsek, with scary rapids," Marie replied, trying to make her friend laugh.

"Ten days with Mr. Robertson, who thinks all girls are in need of protection, paddling with Charles who never stops boasting, and camping with Belinda who believes she will be Canada's first female hockey star. No, I really don't look forward to the trip even if there are exciting rapids."

"Maybe there'll be other students who you'll get along with even better than me. After all, I am not exactly the bravest white-water rafter you've paddled with," Marie said.

"I don't care that you get a little nervous when we hit the big stuff. It's your upbringing. Your grandma told you from the day you crawled that you must be careful. Even last summer in North Fork she was still telling you not to fall in the river when you walked along the bank. Not exactly required advice for a fourteen year old. Instead, she should be warning you about the dangers of boys."

"You should be warned of the dangers of being too mouthy with boys."

"And just what do you mean by that remark, Marie?"

"Just that, well, I know you make rude remarks to the boys you like the most."

"I don't like any boys. Most of them are just too clumsy and they're stupid in school. Besides, that dunce Billy teased me yesterday because you're my friend."

"I know. I heard him. *Going out with the breeds are you? Next you'll be wearing skins and eating gophers.* I reported him to the Native

Learning Assistant and he'll be in trouble. There's no room for people like him anymore."

"I have to give you credit, Marie. I wouldn't have dared to say anything because it just seems to make the teasing worse."

"My grandma told me to stand up for myself. She said that I have only been used to a small Indian village where everyone looks after me and that when I am in the big city without my own people it is up to me to speak up for my rights. That is what I am going to do all the way through to graduation."

"How come you didn't speak up when your parents wouldn't let you go on the rafting trip?"

"Julianna, you know I have to do as my parents ask. Maybe you argue with your mother, but I can't. Besides, while you're away, my other grandmother—the one who is Tlingit—will be visiting and she promised to teach me how to weave Chilkat blankets."

"White-water rafting is more appealing to me. I've never had much patience for handicrafts," Julianna admitted.

Julianna and Marie had been inseparable since grade five, spending their summers together and sharing all their holidays. A trip without Marie was not something Julianna could get excited about. She even pleaded with Marie's parents to change their minds. It was no use. They remained firm.

"Do you want me to come and help you pack?"

"That would help get me out of my funk. Thanks, Marie."

Early Saturday morning Julianna and Marie waited outside the junior high school. The day was clear and unusually warm for early May.

"You're even going to have sunny weather. Aren't you getting excited?" Marie asked.

"I don't feel right about this trip. My parents have always taken me on white-water trips, and I'm a little nervous about paddling with anyone else."

"Don't worry about Mr. Robertson. I'm sure he is capable of leaping over the water as well as paddling upstream. He may be an obnoxious jerk, but he's got to be the strongest Outdoor Ed teacher we've ever had."

"But Marie, there is more to white water than muscle. One of the best female kayakers in Whitehorse was disabled by polio, but when she's in the big waves she's better than a lot of the young kayakers."

"At least Mr. Robertson prepared the Outdoor Education class well enough to make a trip to the North Pole—sleeping in snow caves, rock climbing and ski trips through blizzards. The river trip should be a breeze after those adventures. And he's always brought everyone home safe," Marie contended.

"Although he may be as strong as Schwartzenegger, I sometimes worry about his judgement. He never listens to anyone. Remember when you tried to tell him that a storm was on the way, and he laughed at you? And speaking of big and tough. Here he comes," Julianna said.

A van pulled into the parking lot and a tall, heavy but muscular man in his mid-thirties jumped from the driver's seat. He was followed by a lanky native boy who waved at Julianna and smiled.

"Hey, Julianna, isn't that your old boyfriend, Graham?" Marie asked. Julianna ran her fingers nervously through her blond hair and then turned away, pretending she had not seen him.

"There you go again, ignoring someone you like," Marie scolded.

"We don't talk to each other anymore," Julianna explained. "He's changed since he became one of the chosen few to ski in Europe last year. He wouldn't even go with our family on our river trip last summer."

"Have it your way, Julianna, but just maybe he had a good reason for not going. Anyway, you two will certainly have to talk to each other. This trip is up close and personal and it will be pretty hard to avoid each other."

"Don't expect me to bring any good news stories back," Julianna warned. "Wow! Look at the gear Belinda's got! That's enough for five rafters!" A tall, athletic girl threw her heavy pack into the van.

"That must be Jenny," Marie said, as they watched a small native girl struggle with her pack. "She's related to my Grandmother and I heard she would be on this trip."

"Okay gang, let's get your gear into the van," Mr. Robertson's voice boomed out. "Hop to it gals!"

"All right, all right," Julianna said to herself. "I can hear you." She picked up her big green water-tight gear bag, swung it onto her shoulder, lifted her day bag and paddle, and heaved all her gear into the back of the van.

"See you in ten days, Marie," she called out as the van pulled out from the school parking lot. The group made another stop to pick up Ms. Lindsay, the Science teacher, before heading down the highway to the beginning of the river trip.

Two hours later, the van pulled into the Kluane Park Visitors' Center.

"Pile out you kids," Mr. Robertson ordered. "Ten minutes for a pee break and we'll be on our way to the river."

"Mr. Robertson, can we look at the park film?" Julianna asked. "They show slides of Mt. Logan and the glaciers and…"

"Look, gal," Mr. Robertson interrupted, "that might be interesting but we're here to be outdoors, not spend our time in a movie theatre. I said ten minutes and I mean ten minutes."

It was a little longer. Ms. Lindsay was attracted to the displays in the visitors' centre. The most interesting feature was a three-dimensional model of the park, showing the highest mountain range in Canada and glaciers that stretched to the Alaskan coastline. She called the students over to look at the route they would take.

As they approached the huge map, they noticed a young man in his early twenties staring at the model. He was dressed in expensive, foreign-looking outdoor clothing.

"Gary, I find the model very helpful," Ms. Lindsay explained to Mr. Robertson. "After all, I just arrived in the Yukon a few months ago so my knowledge of the Alsek River is pretty limited. If I am going to teach the students about the area, I will need a little more than the text books I brought along."

"Look Mr. Robertson! The Alsek goes into a narrow canyon. Are we going through there?" Julianna asked, apprehensive at handling the white water with this group.

"No, you can't go through the canyon. It's too dangerous." The man leaning over the model spoke to Julianna in perfect English, but with a strong German accent. "You must get a plane and fly over. It's called Turnback Canyon and only the best kayakers do that. I am not even sure I will go without swimming."

"We're starting on the river today," Julianna said.

"Who leads you on this trip?" the young man asked.

"My Outdoor Ed teacher, Mr. Robertson. He has probably arranged for a plane. He hasn't told us too much about the trip except that we will become tougher. Mr. Robertson, you should talk to…," Julianna paused and turned to the young man. "What is your name?"

"Dietmar Schern…," he began to stutter as he tried to say his last name. "Uh, uh, Schernernberger."

Charles punched Graham in the side and smirked. "Hey listen, he stutters just like you used to."

The German visitor heard this and looked away, embarrassed.

Graham's face turned red, and he moved away from Charles to join Julianna, who was studying the map.

Julianna continued, "Mr. Robertson, Dietmar says we must have a plane to go over the canyon."

"Don't worry about the trip, Julianna, I have it under control. Do me a favour and don't listen to the first stranger you talk to." Then, turning to Dietmar, he asked, "And what do you know about our rivers? Aren't you pretty new here?"

"Yes, I come from Germany to paddle your beautiful waters and I have read about this river. I am looking for a group to go with. The park officials will not let me go alone. I wonder if I could come with you? I can be a rescue boat in case the river is too big and the raft goes over. What you think?" the German asked.

"Well, I have never even come close to flipping a raft," Mr. Robertson asserted. "But you're right about needing a rescue kayak. The girls don't have the muscle to hold on when the raft bounces. So you're welcome to come. I know there is more food on this trip than we need."

"That is really very kind of you, but I will also bring my own food. I will get my gear ready very fast." The young German smiled and headed for the door and then paused to add, "I will put my kayak on top of your van."

"Gary, I need to talk to you alone," Ms. Lindsay said, motioning Mr. Robertson over to the other side of the room. "Are you sure it's wise to bring someone we know nothing about? Maybe he won't get along with us and we will have nothing but conflicts for the entire trip."

"You sound like you just arrived from the big city where everyone you meet is a potential murderer. Well, I didn't take too much risk. I heard some of the kayakers talk about this German fellow, saying he was the best kayaker they've ever seen. I'm sure he is the same guy because they said he had a stutter. Besides, if you get eaten in a big hole, you may be very glad he's there to pull you and your students out of the water."

"What makes you think I can't handle the big water? You sound like the male chauvinists I hoped to leave behind in Toronto."

"Well, I'm from the old school. So I don't really mind if you straighten me out once in a while, just as long as you do what I say when we are in the dangerous sections of the river."

"Maybe you should follow me through the canyon or maybe we should follow the kayaker."

"That young guy who's still wet behind the ears? He may be a super kayaker, but I wouldn't follow him across a pond. Speaking of the youth, here he is. Okay, gang, time to head for the wet stuff!"

Soon they arrived at the river and began loading up the rafts. Graham stood beside Julianna as the students passed the gear from the shore and onto the rafts.

"Before you bite my head off, Juje, I just wanted to tell you that I am glad you're on this trip because at least you know how to paddle in white water. Remember the trips we took on the Nisutlin when we were in grade four?" Graham asked.

"That was an eon ago, and everything has changed since then. And don't call me that baby name," Julianna snapped. "I'm called Julianna." She wanted to apologize to Graham for being so abrupt, but couldn't get the words out. Instead, she continued with her biting tone. "If you want to know, I hated every moment of those trips," she said.

"Why do you have to say things like that?" Graham's irritation was evident.

"What things?" Julianna couldn't leave it be.

"Okay Julianna, have it your way. I just don't know about

you anymore."

"Time for the group photo," Ms. Lindsay announced, grabbing her camera bag. "Please get on one raft and I will run over just in time for the shot." She placed the camera on a stump and scrambled onto the raft before the shutter clicked.

"Would you wait for me to take a picture?" the German asked. "And would you photograph me in my kayak so I have a picture to give to my girlfriend in Germany?"

"We better get going here, so hurry up with this picture taking," Mr. Robertson announced, impatient with the delays. "Everyone put on your helmets and lifejackets."

The students wore splash pants and windbreakers. Julianna, who had been on many river trips with her family, wore a lifejacket with a knife encased in a special pocket in the jacket and a pouch at the back that held her first-aid and emergency supplies.

The two rafts pushed out into the current, with the kayaker following. Jenny, Belinda and Charles were on the raft with Ms. Lindsay. Julianna and Graham were with Mr. Robertson. The two teachers handled the big rowing oars while the students were occasionally asked to help with the standard paddles.

"Ms. Lindsay, are there salmon in this river?" Jenny asked.

"No, the salmon all run up the Tatshenshini River to spawn in the little creeks."

"But I thought we were on the Tatshenshini River," Jenny said.

"Wow, are you confused!" Charles laughed. "Don't you know Mr. Robertson changed the trip from the Tat to the Alsek? He told me the Indian band checks all the groups entering the Tat, and that he had a problem with the permit."

"I thought he had always planned to do this river and that he had been down the Alsek several times," Ms. Lindsay said.

"Well, Mr. Robertson told me lots of his friends have been down the Alsek and that it was easier to raft than the Tat. He's guided for Outdoor Adventures on the biggest rivers in the North. He knows what he's doing."

"We could be heading for Niagara Falls for all I know," the teacher confessed, "so I'm glad Mr. Robertson is leading this trip."

"How about you, Ms. Lindsay? What kind of rivers have you done?" Charles asked.

"I started canoeing when I was ten, and have been rafting for the last five years."

"A canoe! Mr. Robertson calls that a pig boat," Charles teased. "That's for sissies!"

"And do you know what canoeists call rafts? Cattle boats," Ms. Lindsay retorted with a laugh. "And rafters are called raftoids, because instead of paddling steady, they talk all the time. Now what is it you wanted to say about canoeing?"

"If you haven't been down white water in a raft, I think I'll change to Mr. Robertson's raft."

"Don't jump overboard yet, Charles. I can handle the big waves," Ms. Lindsay claimed.

"We'll see. Right now I hope Mr. Robertson will pull over and let us have lunch. I'm starving," Charles announced. "I'll give him a whistle." The sound pierced the valley.

"Ouch! Don't you think you should just use that for emergencies?" Jenny complained with her hands over her ears.

Mr. Robertson looked back and Charles pointed his finger at his mouth and rubbed his stomach.

"Okay, I get the message," Mr. Robertson yelled as he pulled on the oars and steered for a nearby eddy.

The sun had warmed the sandy beach and shone down on the lunch spot.

"I wish I had my bathing suit under all these clothes so I could get a sun tan. Look at Dietmar. He certainly doesn't worry about how many clothes he takes off," Belinda remarked, grinning at Julianna and Jenny.

Jenny was too embarrassed to look at the young man. Julianna glanced at the skimpily clad German, then blushed when she saw Graham watching her. Belinda kept looking at Dietmar and then began to giggle. Ms. Lindsay heard her and, realizing that the German's bathing suit was the cause of the amusement, signalled Belinda to be silent.

I'll have to tell Dietmar that he has to wear more clothes around the teenage girls, she thought. She said, "He comes from another country where there is much less restraint. To him, it is very natural. To us, it is considered inappropriate. We must pay no attention."

"Okay, Ms. Lindsay, if you say so," Belinda replied with a mischievous grin.

Turning to Julianna, she added in a whisper, "Don't you think Ms. Lindsay will have more trouble ignoring his beautiful muscles than we will?"

Julianna was beginning to enjoy Belinda's boldness, thinking that, unlike herself, the outspoken teenager said exactly what was on her mind.

"I'm having trouble ignoring Graham. He's real cute, don't you think?" Belinda asked, unaware that Julianna and Graham were once childhood playmates.

"I guess he is. So are you setting out to catch him?" Julianna asked, trying to hide her irritation at the prospect of Graham falling for Belinda.

"Hey, don't bite my head off. It looks like you have a thing for Graham," Belinda replied.

"What? No way, I can't stand him anymore, but we used to be friends. Now he's letting his school work slide and can't think of anything but skiing."

"I am not hiring for a job so I don't pick boys on the basis of their marks," Belinda laughed. "In fact, the boys who make straight As are sometimes the nerds in the class."

"I guess some people think I am a nerd because I like school and get pretty good marks," Julianna responded.

It was time to get underway. The group picked up their gear and loaded up the rafts.

"Mr. Robertson, would it be all right if I traded places with Julianna?" Charles asked.

"Sure, jump in for now, but when we reach the first set of rapids Ms. Lindsay will need a strong boy to help keep her off the rock walls."

"Gary," Ms. Lindsay said, taking Mr. Robertson aside, "I am not exactly a weakling. Besides, I think Julianna is just as capable as Charles."

"You females are pretty sensitive, aren't you?"

"Some of the men need to become SNAGS."

"SNAGS! Now let me in on that one."

"Sensitive New Age Guys. Definitely something you have not heard of and something we should both be passing on to the boys on this trip."

"Well, I intend to show them how to survive in the wilderness, not date girls," Mr. Robertson replied.

"You're impossible—but I have to admit you know a few things about the outdoors, so maybe I will focus on teaching sensitivity and you can show them how to chop down trees with a single blow."

"You're making me out to be a lot worse than I am. It'll work out okay, Marina, you'll see," Mr. Robertson said before turning to the students. "All right, you kids! Load'er up and let's get motoring. Charles, do you want to take a turn at rowing?"

"Sure thing, Mr. Robertson."

Towards the end of the day, the river flattened out as they neared Lowell Lake and gale-force winds blew down against the little group. The headwind was so strong that it felt as if they were trying to paddle upstream. Ms. Lindsay, Jenny, Julianna and Belinda struggled to keep the raft moving forward. Even Mr. Robertson, despite his considerable strength, was barely able to keep the raft moving downstream.

As the winds increased in force, Ms. Lindsay's energy dwindled. "This is just too much!" She lifted her paddle to signal to Mr. Robertson to pull out of the river. However, instead of pulling over, he gave the signal to continue.

"Okay kids, I guess we're in for another hour of torture. Grab your paddles, girls. I'll keep working on the oars, but I need your help if we are to make any progress."

They continued for another hour, then stopped briefly for water and a snack. The raft drifted back upstream.

"Paddle, girls. If we don't work harder we'll never get to our campsite." They picked up their paddles with hands that were sore and cold.

As they moved slowly forward, Dietmar paddled alongside. "Would you like me to help with the rowing?" he asked Ms. Lindsay. "You are getting too tired now and Mr. Robertson is far ahead."

"Yes, please. I could use a break," she said with relief. "I didn't know you could row. From now on, you take the rowing frame and I'll kayak."

"You don't get to quit. But I will help you row. Would you young women please tie my kayak to the raft?" Dietmar asked, before lifting himself out of the kayak and jumping nimbly onto the raft. "I rowed when I was young guy and needed to earn money for school. Here, you stand on one side of the oars and I will take the other. Then it will be easy."

"Nothing is easy. But at least this feels better. Thank you. I guess I should have refused help and pretended to be tough," Ms. Lindsay said. "Girls, you won't rat on me and tell Mr. Robertson that I needed help, will you?"

"Never in your life, Ms. Lindsay," Julianna promised.

"Your secret is safe with us," Belinda laughed.

"I'll bribe you by giving you girls a ten-minute break from the paddling."

Jenny, Belinda and Julianna shielded their faces from the wind and curled up for a rest. In an hour, the wind abated and the rowing frame sped through the water.

"Look, there's the shoreline of Old Lake Alsek," Julianna remarked, pointing high up on the surrounding mountain side.

"What did you say—an old lake?" Dietmar inquired.

"The lines on the side of the mountain are made from the shores of a lake," Julianna explained. "I don't know too much about it except there was a huge lake here a long time ago."

"I read a little about the glacier lakes," Ms. Lindsay added in between strokes with the oars. "About two hundred years ago the Lowell Glacier surged, or moved down the valley, and blocked the river. This ice dam created a giant lake that covered all this area past the place where we started on the river. Then about one hundred years ago the ice dam gave way and released the lake water, and the Alsek became a big river again."

"If I had been there in my kayak, I would have had fun in the big waves when the water flooded through the valley," Dietmar laughed.

"It wasn't funny," Jenny said. The paddlers were surprised to hear Jenny add to the conversation, especially to contradict someone. "Remember, we were asked to research our family history before coming on the trip, especially if our ancestors were living in this area. Well, I talked to my Granny who will be one hundred years old this year. She told me that a long time ago her family lived around this area when the dam burst. There were young men in boats that were swept away in the water and were drowned. An entire village downstream was flooded, and several of the people lost their lives. She said that some of Graham's relatives lived in that flooded village."

"I must apologize. Please excuse me for making fun. It was a poor thing for a visitor to say. I–I am sorry." Dietmar was clearly taken aback by Jenny's story.

"It's okay," Jenny said.

"Maybe you would bring me to see your grandmother someday," Ms. Lindsay said. "I would love to meet her."

"She taught me how to sew moccasins, and now I want to be sewing even when I am floating down the river," Jenny explained in her soft voice.

The others wanted to hear more about Jenny's people. However, Ms. Lindsay did not want to drop too far behind Mr. Robertson's raft.

"I have to ask you girls to grab your paddles again so we can catch up to the other raft," she said.

"Would you like me to sing a song to speed us over the water?" Dietmar asked.

They all nodded, happy for any distraction from the wearisome toil.

"I will sing about a poor boy who lost his sweetheart and wandered the world searching for her. He went through dangerous waters and died, then he joined his loved one in the next world."

He sang in German in a soft melodious voice. As he sang, Julianna noticed a deep sadness fall upon his face. *Yes,* she thought, *there is something troubling him.* The song took their minds off the pain in their tired muscles.

With two people at the oars, they eventually caught up to the other raft. At six that evening they reached their campsite and began setting up tents and preparing the evening meal.

The midnight sun kept the group from even thinking about bedtime. It was so bright that Julianna was able to write in her diary till after 10 p.m. Later, when everyone gathered about the fire, Ms. Lindsay asked Julianna to relate what she had learned of her family history.

"Well, I don't have any history for this river, but my mother's family came over the Chilkoot Pass during the Klondike Goldrush. My mother's great-grandfather came first. He made a small income as a teacher. He heard about the Forty Mile gold rush and then was lucky to learn about the Klondike strike in 1896 when he was mining a few hours downriver from where Skookum Jim and his friends found the big strike. He managed to get to Dawson City when there was still good ground to be staked."

She continued, "He left his wife, Sarah, and their young son with his mother-in-law at home. His luck did not last. He died soon after writing his family about his rich claim. We don't know all of the story. I think his wife died and the grandmother travelled with the ten-year-old boy, crossed the Chilkoot and reached the Klondike to take over the mining property. She must have been a very determined woman."

"Hey, you made that up," Charles said. "Your family is not rich at all. If you had a Klondike gold property, you would be a millionaire."

"You're right. We aren't wealthy, but I know my grandfather was born in Dawson and he was the son of the ten-year-old boy who came over the pass. Anyway, that's my story."

"My family only came to the Yukon in 1980," Belinda announced. "They were store keepers in Manitoba since the middle of the nineteenth century."

"I guess we have something in common," Charles added. "My family were store keepers as well. That is, they were saloon keepers in Skagway around the time of the gold rush. Actually, they were a little on the crooked side according to my dad. My mother never lets him talk about great-grandfather, so the story is a deep family secret."

"Hey, I believe your family were crooks," Belinda laughed.

"And a history I am proud of," Charles said with good humour.

"I guess that's enough history for tonight," Ms. Lindsay said. "I know it's still light out but it's time to turn in."

"Hold on," Mr. Robertson said. "I want to go over technique for the white-water section that we will hit tomorrow. First, I think Charles and Belinda should go with Ms. Lindsay to give her some extra muscle power. Julianna and Graham, I guess you two have been on the water before, but you're both a bit skinny, so you should come with me."

"What about me?" Jenny's voice was so quiet that Mr. Robertson did not hear her.

"I'd like you to come with me, Jenny," Ms. Lindsay said.

"Oh, yeh, you take Jenny. That will give you one more person to paddle," Mr. Robertson replied. "When we reach the rapids I'd like everyone to get into your footholds, and sit inside the raft. I noticed you kids dragging a leg over the side today. Do that in the big water and you might just go for a swim. When we go over a roller, the raft will buck and try to send you flying. I want you to grab the safety line, and I will keep paddling. You hang on, cause I don't want to lose anyone. Now if you fall out, don't panic. Float on your back with your feet downstream. If you can grab the raft, make sure you don't get on the downstream side and get mashed between the raft and a cliff wall."

"I will be right there if you swim," Dietmar added. "I will place the back of the kayak near you and you must grab the loop. Then, I will pull you to shore."

"'Sam' and 'Bill' are not just rapids, they are holes, so expect to eat some white stuff," Mr. Robertson cautioned.

Jenny was puzzled, because she couldn't visualize a hole in the river. "What will it look like?" she asked.

"When the fast water hits a big rock or drops over a ledge, the water on the downriver side circulates upstream. It looks like a giant hole in the river," Julianna explained. Turning to Mr. Robertson, she added, "Don't you think you should tell everyone how to paddle through a hole in case we can't miss it?" Julianna asked.

"I don't intend to miss the hole," Mr. Robertson replied. "What fun would that be? We go right through the middle, but don't you kids worry. I will keep the raft's momentum and we will be through the hole before you can take a breath."

"I would like some help in my raft," Ms. Lindsay said. "We'll skirt the hole, but if we miss and go in, I want you to dig your paddles into the water in front of the raft and help me bring the boat out of the hole and into the water flowing downstream. Make sure you are solidly in the footholds, then lean out into the water and use a high downstream brace, like this." Ms. Lindsay demonstrated with a paddle, positioning her arms and body expertly.

Dietmar watched. "That is very perfect. You must be a good raft guide with much experience, right?"

"I guided on the Ottawa River and never had a client go for a swim, but once on my own I flipped a rowing frame in a big hole so I know how strong the hydraulics are." She smiled at Dietmar, pleased that someone recognized she had the necessary skill to be a raft guide.

"Never flipped yet," Mr. Robertson bragged, "and never will."

"There are two kinds of rafting guides, ones that have flipped and guides that soon may flip," Dietmar said, repeating the often-quoted phrase of experienced rafters. "I think it is better to be like Ms. Lindsay. She already flipped her raft and now maybe it's your turn."

"Good story, my German friend, but you are dead wrong."

"What do you mean about me being dead?" Dietmar asked, not understanding the expression.

"It's just a saying. He did not mean that you were going to die," Ms. Lindsay explained.

"My friends told me that I will die in the river some day because I always tempt 'Woton' the water god. They say that when I was caught in a hole, I talked to the water and stroked the waves until I got out."

"I will try that tomorrow if I get into trouble in Big Sam," Ms. Lindsay laughed. "And now my little water frogs, it is midnight and time for the sack. Who's doing breakfast tomorrow?"

"Oh no, it's Jenny. I suppose you will take two hours to burn the pancakes or overcook the porridge," Charles teased.

"It's definitely time for you to retire, Charles, and before you go, please apologize to Jenny. You have no reason to suggest she cannot cook."

"Ms. Lindsay is right, Charles. Smarten up," Mr. Robertson said sharply.

"Okay, okay. I didn't really mean it. I was just kidding."

However, as Charles had said, the next morning Jenny took two hours to cook breakfast but everything she prepared was perfect.

"With this tasty meal in our innards, it will be tough to get moving," Mr. Robertson remarked, "but we're late, so let's load up the rafts and head for the rapids."

CHAPTER 2

RUNNING THE RAPIDS

There was a stretch of quiet water before the beginning of the rapids. Rounding a curve in the river, Julianna could see the rocky walls. The river entered a series of riffles, curving around sharply into rolling waves. Mr. Robertson stood in the raft looking downriver to choose his path and calling out the directions to Julianna and Graham. "Hard right, back paddle, LEFT, LEFT!" Then ahead the river flattened out for a few metres before dropping over a ledge. Julianna could see the turbulent water spraying in rooster tails and boils. They headed for the centre of the ledge.

"HOLD ON!" The raft dropped over the ledge. Julianna could see the hole below them, so big that she thought it would swallow the raft. She dug her paddle into the aerated water to help Mr. Robertson bring the raft through. Graham clung to the safety line and jammed his feet into the supports, ready for the impact. The raft plunged down the ledge, engulfing Julianna and Graham in foam and almost throwing them into the water. The raft powered through the hole, up the surging water and into the downstream current. Julianna was exhilarated by the white water and could not contain herself.

"Hey, that was awesome! Wasn't it, Graham?" Julianna cried out.

"It was a blast and you're even better at paddling than I remember," Graham replied.

"Thanks," Julianna said. Then, before she could stop herself, she added, "You would be good, too, if you didn't spend all your time training to be the world's next Bjorn Dahly or whoever that super Swedish skier is."

"Still the same sour tune, eh Julianna? And anyway, he's Norwegian," Graham retorted.

Mr. Robertson turned the raft sideways so they could watch Ms. Lindsay come through the rapids. She entered far right of the hole, aiming at a spot just right of a mid-river boulder. It was a good line that would keep her raft away from the hole.

As she entered the rapids, Ms. Lindsay explained her approach. "We'll just miss that rock, give it a little bounce and it will spin us into a clean path down the boulder run. Be ready to paddle when I call." But the roar of the water drowned out her words.

The raft moved slowly down the less turbulent route. Charles and Belinda spotted the mid-river rock directly ahead. "The rock, Ms. Lindsay! WATCH OUT!" Charles yelled.

"It's okay. We're on line." But again, her voice was lost in the roar of the water.

Mr. Robertson watched from below as the raft headed for the mid-river boulder. "What the hell? She's headed right for the rock."

"I think she's using the rock to spin on. My dad and mom do that all the time," Julianna said.

"I think you're right, Julianna," Graham added encouragingly.

Mr. Robertson didn't listen to Julianna. Instead, he grabbed Julianna's paddle and signalled that the group in the other raft should go left.

Charles saw the signal and passed on the message to Belinda, who sat close to him at the back of the raft. "Mr. Robertson wants us to go left. We're not going to clear the rock if we go right."

The raft was close to the boulder when Ms. Lindsay gave the call: "RIGHT! RIGHT! HARD!"

Charles and Belinda looked at Mr. Robertson's wild gestures. Charles shook his head and motioned to Belinda to paddle left.

Ms. Lindsay struggled with the oars trying to pull the raft right. Meanwhile, Charles and Belinda paddled in the opposite direction. The raft headed directly for the boulder and jammed on the rock.

"We're stuck. Kids, move over here!" Ms. Lindsay jumped to the right side of the raft to release the weight against the rock. Charles, Belinda and Jenny sat like zombies. "Get over here or we'll get pinned!" she yelled. Jenny moved over. "ALL OF YOU! QUICK!" She grabbed Charles's collar and dragged him over. Belinda followed. As the weight got distributed, the raft swung free of the rock and plunged down through the rapids. Ms. Lindsay grabbed the oars and brought the boat into the eddy beside Mr. Robertson. She was furious.

"What do you think you were doing, interfering with my calls?" she yelled at Mr. Robertson. "And you two," Ms. Lindsay said, glaring at Charles and Belinda, "don't you ever disobey my raft calls again!"

"You were heading for the rock. You should have gone left. There was lots of room to miss the hole," Mr. Robertson argued.

"Maybe I didn't want to get near the hole. I knew what I was doing, and I do not appreciate having someone override my instructions."

The kayaker pulled up beside the rafts and listened to the angry exchange. "The next rapid will come up soon. I will be at the bottom in the eddy. In the book it said that the second rapid is called 'Bill' and is not so hard."

Mr. Robertson handled the oars, and Julianna and Graham made certain their feet were firmly in the footholds as their raft led the way into the next difficult section where the river took a sharp turn.

Mr. Robertson took the raft too close to the wall. One pontoon was already underwater, and the side of the raft nearest the cliff tipped almost straight up.

"High-side!" Julianna yelled at Graham. Immediately, Graham moved to the canyon side of the raft. The two young people threw their weight towards the cliff as Mr. Robertson strained on the oars trying to keep the raft from flipping.

"PUSH HARD!" Julianna commanded. Both of them jammed their paddles against the cliff wall and leaned towards the rock. Slowly, the raft dropped off the wall and pillowed away from the dangerous corner. They were still on board.

"Julianna, what do you think you were doing?" Mr. Robertson yelled. He was obviously shaken by the close call.

Julianna was stunned by his angry tone. "I–I–," she couldn't think of what to say.

"She just saved our skins, in case you didn't notice," Graham retorted.

"We were just fine," Mr. Robertson scolded. "Next time you kids stay in the footholds. You could have been thrown in the water. Don't ever do that again!"

"We won't, Mr. Robertson," Graham replied, then winked

at Julianna.

Julianna smiled back, happy at having Graham stick up for her.

Upstream, Ms. Lindsay took a few minutes to strap down the gear before beginning her run through the rapids.

"Did you see that?" Belinda asked. "I thought they were going to swim!"

"He was okay," Ms. Lindsay added. "It looks like he gave Graham and Julianna the correct instructions and they righted the raft in time. I have seen a commercial guide and all his clients get flipped on a sharp curve just like this. The raft started to climb the wall until it was standing straight up against the cliff, then it tipped and everyone got dumped out."

"Will we be okay?" Belinda asked, apprehensive after watching her schoolmates nearly get thrown into the rapids.

"Just follow my instructions this time," Ms. Lindsay cautioned. "All right kids, here we go!"

They left the eddy and plunged into the rapids speeding towards the sharp turn. The waves pillowed against the canyon wall.

"RIGHT! RIGHT! HARD!" The three students dug their paddles into the water. Ms. Lindsay strained on the oars, positioning the boat perfectly. The raft glided along the canyon walls at an angle, bouncing over the waves but never touching the wall.

The lunch break started out dismally. Ms. Lindsay took out her book while Julianna put out the food.

"I'm sorry, there's only water to drink. I forgot to bring the juice crystals."

"I just love drinking water filled with silt," Belinda complained.

"But it does keep you regular," Mr. Robertson said, trying to get the group to lighten up. "Have you heard that if you drink glacier water you'll get the runs?"

"Man, I could use a glass of milk straight from the fridge," Charles said, sipping a cup of gray, sandy water.

"Or a chocolate milkshake from McDonald's," Belinda laughed.

"A malt from Riverside," Julianna said.

"A slurpy from Tags," Jenny chimed in.

"A beer from Cheers," Mr. Robertson added.

"Yes, I agree," Ms. Lindsay said, finally smiling at the group.

"And to the whole group, I want to apologize to Ms. Lindsay for telling her how to run the rapids. I've learned my lesson and will not cross her again," Mr. Robertson said, smiling at Ms. Lindsay.

"You'd better not or you'll be in serious trouble. But for now, I forgive you, just this once."

They camped early that night. Tomorrow, they would enter the canyon and Mr. Robertson wanted the students to be well rested. The angry exchange between the two leaders was put aside and the group sat around the campfire recounting the excitement of the run through the rapids.

There was a more serious conversation between Ms. Lindsay and the kayaker.

"I am writing about th–th–this night because tomorrow it will be very dangerous for the students," Dietmar said with concern. "Turnback Canyon has taken one life already and is the most difficult water I will ever kayak. It is bigger than th–th–the Colorado that I kayaked last summer."

"Are you sure about this?" Ms. Lindsay asked. "Mr. Robertson tells me that trips go down the Alsek every week."

"Sure th–th–they go down the Alsek but all fly around th–th–the canyon. Turnback is known around the world to the kayakers who want to take a big chance. It is not a trip for students, only for the very best white-water kayakers, not even for r–r–"

"Rafts." Ms. Lindsay finished Dietmar's sentence. "My God, does Gary know this?"

"I–I–I tried to tell him several times but he didn't listen to me. He thinks a foreigner does not know these things," Dietmar replied. "No matter what we say, he will go through the canyon tomorrow."

"If he wants to go, he can risk his life but he should not endanger the students. I am not going on. I can tell you that for sure."

"Why didn't you bring a radio so you could call for a helicopter?" Dietmar asked.

"Once we are in the mountains, we are out of range," Ms. Lindsay explained.

"Then I think you have to portage around the canyon with the students. They will find it hard going, but if you stay back from the canyon it is quite safe."

"What about you? Will you go through the canyon?"

"Mr. Robertson should not go alone. I–I will lead through the canyon and be there in case there is trouble. Maybe I will swim because the water is very high now. Most kayakers go through in September when the water is lower, not in the spring. I read that kayakers cannot roll their kayaks in sections of the canyon because the waves are as big as in the ocean."

"You will be risking your life to help us," Ms. Lindsay said with concern.

"I am not afraid of dying in the canyon. When this trip ends, I leave behind this beautiful river. I am worried about the students."

Julianna overheard Dietmar. "You mean you wouldn't mind if you drowned in the canyon? Why would you think that way?"

"Maybe I should not have said that. I will try to explain. You see, I have little to go back to in Germany. When I go home, I must save money for a house and a family and I may never kayak again. I will go back to live in a country with polluted rivers and smog. That is no life for me."

"But you have a girlfriend," Ms. Lindsay said.

"No, I broke up with my girlfriend because I always want to be on the river and she only liked to stay at home. I wanted the picture in case I find a girlfriend when I return. Then, I would show her the photo of me kayaking in the wilderness and she would understand what kind of man I am."

"Why didn't she come with you?" Julianna asked, unable to understand why anyone would not want to kayak with Dietmar.

"I guess I should have a girlfriend like Ms. Lindsay who is an expert in the white water," Dietmar smiled.

Of course he would think of Ms. Lindsay as a girlfriend even if she is a couple of years older than he is, Julianna thought, turning away from the group with a hurt look. *He is certainly not going to pay any attention to a stupid fourteen year old.*

Realizing he had injured Julianna's feelings, Dietmar added, "Maybe

I will come back when you are a young woman, Julianna, because you will be an amazing kayaker."

Julianna smiled. "Sure," she said, immediately cheered, "I'll expect you in the twenty-first century when I am twenty-one. I have to turn in now." Her injured feelings assuaged, she left for her tent.

The fire burned down to red coals. From the tents Ms. Lindsay and Dietmar heard a sleepy voice.

"That's Julianna. She also talked in her sleep last night," Ms. Lindsay explained.

Julianna had fallen into an uneasy sleep. She could see Lake Alsek before the flood. An old woman stood on the shoreline, her hands clasped to her chest. Her voice wavered, "You must not travel on the river. There is great danger for you. It is too warm and there will be ice and water flooding you. You must listen to your grandma. I know what I tell you."

A teenage boy approached the old woman. He put his arms around her and kissed her wrinkled cheek.

"Don't worry Grandma. You–you–," he stuttered, "know I have been down the river many times and always I come back safe. I will bring you a warm blanket."

He joined his two companions who were loading furs into three large dug-out boats.

In her dream, Julianna saw the three boats glide out into the water. The sun was so dazzling that it disturbed her sleep. She muttered, "Listen to your grandma."

Julianna woke feeling weary from her disturbing dream. She rolled up her sleeping bag and joined Ms. Lindsay at the campfire.

"It's my day to cook, and I'm going to make chocolate chip pancakes just like my dad makes," she announced.

"I think Mr. Robertson is anxious to get on the river, so I'll give you a hand if you like," Ms. Lindsay offered.

Mr. Robertson also offered to help. "I always like to help the little ladies, so can I fetch you a load of wood and help with the fire?" he asked.

Julianna bristled at being called a "little lady," but held her tongue. "I would sure appreciate a good fire. Not big flames, but hot coals with a steady heat. That's the way my dad likes the fire when he makes pancakes."

When Mr. Robertson headed back for more wood, Ms. Lindsay ran after him. "Gary, can I talk to you about the river? Dietmar told me that the canyon has never been run in a raft and an experienced kayaker drowned in the canyon. I'm really worried about it."

"Look, I never make anyone go if they don't want to. So if you prefer not to do the canyon, that's your choice. The commercial companies do this trip every week, so it can't be a big deal. I'll be going through and if any of the kids want to come with me instead of hiking for ten hours, I'll sure as hell take them." As his voice reached a bellow, Ms. Lindsay realized how pointless it was to argue with him.

"Do as you wish, Mr. Robertson. I intend to make sure the students are safe. I only wish you would be sensible and insist that they all portage the canyon with me."

"I have absolutely no intention of turning them into a flock of sissies. They will come through the canyon if they want and that is the end of the discussion."

Ms. Lindsay was so angry she couldn't speak. Her face burned and her stomach was in knots. "Have it your way, Gaston."

"Gaston? What are you saying?"

"No one can split wood like Gaston; row like Gaston; make fires like Gaston," she sang, paraphrasing the song from *Beauty and the Beast*.

"You're right! So don't try and change me. Okay?"

Ms. Lindsay turned back to the campsite where Julianna offered her a plate of pancakes.

"The pancakes look great, Julianna, but I'm not hungry."

"At least eat one. You'll need some energy if you are going to hike over the glacier," Julianna insisted. "I guess we're changing roles and I'm acting like the teacher."

"I could use some advice about today's events. I am worried about you going through the canyon, and I'm not happy about pulling all our gear on a long portage. You're right, I'd better try and eat."

Ms. Lindsay joined the rest of the group who were seated around the fire.

"I see you spoke with Mr. Robertson and he did not agree with you," Dietmar remarked, "and now you are upset."

"You keep a close watch on all of us, don't you?" Ms. Lindsay replied. "You're right. Mr. Robertson will go through the canyon, but I hope the students will portage across the glacier with me."

"What class is the canyon?" Julianna asked as she continued cooking.

"It is too difficult," Graham said with concern. "You shouldn't go."

"And who's going to stop me?" Julianna replied, trying on her spiky armour once again.

"I guess no one will stop you," Graham said in a resigned tone. "How big is the water, Dietmar?"

"In the guide book for this river, Turnback Canyon is rated Class Six. The kayakers say that is bad and we like bad water. But this is not only difficult water, but dangerous. All the children should go with Ms. Lindsay. Even Mr. Robertson should walk around on the glacier because no raft has ever made it through the canyon."

"Mr. Robertson will go, especially if you tell him it is too difficult. If he goes, Charles will want to be on board, and, although they don't appreciate me, I think Mr. Robertson needs two paddlers to help him through the holes. What do you think, Dietmar?" Julianna asked.

"It—it—it's not good, but I will be there with the kayak to help if you flip. Remember, I am only able to rescue one of you. Don't get in front of the raft or you will get crushed on the canyon walls. I am frightened for you, Julianna, and for Charles and Mr. Robertson, too." Dietmar shook his head.

When Julianna returned to the tent site to pick up her gear, Graham was close behind. "Please don't go. If you go, I will come too. Or maybe you are just going so you can be rescued by the handsome German. Is that right?" Graham said, knowing that Julianna would never back down once she decided to take a risk.

"Come if you like or go with Ms. Lindsay. I really couldn't care less," Julianna replied. "Do you think I am so shallow as to risk my life for such a petty reason?"

Graham had no more to say. He picked up his gear and headed for Mr. Robertson's raft.

Charles was loading on his dry bag and could not contain his excitement at being allowed to go through the canyon with Mr. Robertson. "So, you sissies are just going to walk around while we have all the fun," he teased the others.

"Mr. Robertson, why can't I come with you too?" Belinda asked.

"No, Belinda," Ms. Lindsay interjected. "You're strong but you haven't been through this water level before. Besides, I need help to get the raft across the glacier. I insist you stay with me."

"Ms. Lindsay is right. She'll need you for the portage. I'll take Charles and Julianna, if she's still willing to go," Mr. Robertson said as he tied gear firmly into the raft.

"I'm going through the canyon too," Graham announced.

"No," Ms. Lindsay said. "You don't have much more white-water experience than Belinda."

"Ms. Lindsay, I have to go. You can't stop me if Charles and Julianna are going," Graham argued.

"I want him to come," Mr. Robertson said. "I'll take all the gear through and that will lighten your portage. My motto is to let students reach their potential. If he wants to take the canyon, he can come."

Ms. Lindsay did not have a reply. She walked down to the beach and stared at the entrance to the canyon. *Why can't I just force him to give this up? I have a terrible feeling about this, and once again I am caving in.*

Charles was pleased he did not have to join Ms. Lindsay as he watched Jenny and Belinda struggle up the glacier, tugging the hundred-pound boat and stopping every few minutes to catch their breath. They paused on the glacier and waved.

Mr. Robertson checked the raft to make sure the gear was tightly secured so it would stay on in the rough water.

"This will be a tough stretch of river, so I want you to help me when the raft hits a hole. Can you dig your feet into the footholds and paddle like hell when I need you?"

"I'll try my best, Mr. Robertson." Julianna felt sick at the thought of the dangerous water ahead. *Class Six is too big,* she thought. *The waves will swallow us, and my paddle could get ripped out of my hand like a matchstick. If I swim, I don't know if I will be able to breathe in big water.*

Graham was anxious as they prepared to launch the raft. He turned to Julianna. "Let's stick together if we get into trouble."

"I'm glad you're along," Julianna admitted. These were the first honest words she had spoken to Graham in almost a year.

"Thanks, Julianna," Graham smiled, relieved that the sarcasm was being given a rest.

"We're a team!" Charles yelled confidently.

"That's my boy!" Mr. Robertson answered. He pulled on the oars, sending the raft out into the quiet water. Ahead they could see the narrow entrance to the canyon.

Dietmar's purple kayak led the way to the rocky cliffs.

CHAPTER 3

TURNBACK CANYON

The three students in the raft were all nervous about the approaching danger. Charles concealed his fear by chatting about anything that came into his head. Julianna's stomach churned as she watched the canyon approach. Graham braced himself, hoping he would be able to stay close to Julianna if they tipped. All three gripped their paddles, waiting for Mr. Robertson's instructions.

The current quickened as they entered the canyon. Mr. Robertson strained on the oars as the raft crashed around the first curve of the S-bends.

"Back paddle! Back paddle!" he yelled and the three students dug their paddles in. The raft sped forward towards the steep rocky walls.

"We're going to hit!" Julianna hollered.

"Back! Back!" Mr. Robertson yelled, his voice barely audible above the roar of the rapids.

The raft grazed the cliffs, as the paddlers strained to keep the pontoons from climbing the cliff wall and dumping them.

"HARDER! HARDER!" Mr. Robertson sounded terrified.

The raft held its position, skimming along the rock wall, but not flipping.

"We made it!" Charles let out a whoop.

There was no time to relax. The river made a second sharp turn, throwing the raft towards the left cliff. Once again they strained on the paddles, barely keeping the raft from tearing on the jagged rocks.

"Watch the back end! Push off Julianna!" Mr. Robertson yelled.

Julianna reacted quickly by placing her paddle blade between the sharp rock and the raft.

They hit the canyon wall with a violent impact. Julianna did not lose her grip on the paddle, despite the shot of pain she felt as the shaft of the paddle jabbed into her ribs.

"Good work, Julianna!" Mr. Robertson said tensely. Julianna was aware that the raft might have been torn if she had not acted so quickly.

"We're fine, aren't we, Mr. Robertson?" Charles asked, having sensed that his hero was less than confident about what lay ahead.

"Keep lively mates." There was false enthusiasm in Mr. Robertson's voice.

The turbulence was enormous. Ahead, Dietmar's purple kayak sank into the waves and disappeared in the foam. Mr. Robertson lined up the raft and powered forward, hoping that he could maintain momentum through the towering waves.

"PADDLE HARD! HARD!" The three students tried to dig their paddles into the water, but there was only foam—there was nothing to grip. The raft rose at the bow and sank in the back, covering the young people in icy water. Julianna grabbed the safety line and held tight to her paddle. Graham reached over and held onto Julianna's arm until they surfaced.

"I lost my paddle!" Charles exclaimed.

"Hang on, kids!" Once again the raft plunged into a trough. Julianna felt like she was in the icy rinse cycle of a giant washing machine. She gasped for air and coughed up water when they surfaced. Ahead the river flattened, giving Charles time to grab a spare paddle, and then it narrowed again.

"Oh no!" Julianna exclaimed breathlessly as she saw Dietmar's kayak disappear in the canyon. Just ahead, the Alsek River narrowed to only a few metres. *How can this huge river squeeze through that little opening?* She was terrified at what would happen when the raft reached the slot.

Mr. Robertson could no longer control the raft. He turned to the students and said, "If we flip, for God's sake, try and grab the back end of the raft and keep your feet downstream. Remember, don't be in front of the raft whatever you do!" His voice was strained and filled with fear and desperation.

They were at the gate of the slot. On either side, the cliffs rose straight up from the water. There were no eddies, just a curling snake of boiling water.

"HANG ON!" Mr. Robertson yelled as the raft flushed through

the small passage. It was called the "Hourglass," where the water squeezed through a tiny channel in the canyon. The opening was so small that he had to ship his long oars, bringing them into the raft and leaving him powerless to keep the raft from hitting the canyon walls.

They plunged through the slot, out of control, tossed from one side of the river to the other by the overwhelming force of the water. This section of river had never before been run by a raft. Julianna couldn't bear feeling so helpless. She dug her short canoe paddle into the rapids, hoping she could keep the raft away from the canyon walls. "Right! Right!" she yelled. Graham responded, digging at the water. They sped through the canyon, smashing against the rocky walls, but managing to stay upright.

The raft squeezed out from the slot, and the river widened enough for Mr. Robertson to use the oars. It seemed for a minute as if they had successfully run the worst of the canyon. But ahead the river dropped out of sight. The raft sped over smooth water between the canyon walls, heading for the drop. Julianna was so frightened she could barely speak. She glanced over at Graham and whispered good-bye.

Then over the ledge they went, plunging down into an enormous hole, big enough to swallow a bus. Julianna pushed her feet into the supports in the hope of clinging to the raft and then took a deep breath, preparing to be submerged. The raft was pulled into the hole and she felt herself lifted from her footholds and dragged into the foaming abyss. Her helmet smashed against the rocky cliffs. Then there was only darkness.

CHAPTER 4

OLD LAKE ALSEK

At the headwaters of the Alsek River, an old Tlingit woman cried as she watched three young men pile furs into their dug-out boats.

"Please don't go this time, my grandson. The sun is too hot and is melting the ice. I saw the glacier break in my dream and a young man floating to the ocean. He looked like you, or maybe it was Salkusta, or Kretch. You must stay till the evening when the hot weather is over."

"Don't you worry, Grandma. You always think I will hurt myself but don't I come back every time and bring you pots and knives?"

"There will be no pleasure in all the white man's things if I lose my grandson."

"We will be fine. I will bring you a beautiful blanket to keep you warm this winter." He hugged his grandmother. "Now wish us well. We must go."

The three young men paddled into the lake and disappeared under the ice bridge that separated the lake from the Alsek River. The ice almost blocked off the water, creating a giant lake.

A stream of water poured through the ice bridge, forming the beginning of the Alsek River. Here, the river was so shallow that Kajach-hat and his two companions had to drag their boats across the gravel bars.

"Hey, Kajach-hat, we talk the English now so I can practise. Now I call you Split the Waves. Your grandma not here to tell you speak Tlingit," Salkusta said smiling.

"You speak pretty fine. It's Kretch that needs to learn to speak to the English," Split the Waves replied.

Kretch replied in Tlingit, telling them he had no wish to talk to the devil people that had come from across the ocean to steal their land.

"They are not all bad," Split the Waves said, "and if you understand their English you find out whether or not they are telling the truth. I listen to them when they do not know I can understand them and find out which of the traders I trust and which I stay away from. Smart, eh?"

The three Tlingit boys paddled through calm, shallow water, enjoying the freedom of being away from the Indian camp.

"Hey, what it that noise?" Salkusta asked, looking up to see if there were signs of thunder in the sky.

"No rain, no dark clouds. Maybe the mountains are bringing down rock and snow," Split the Waves suggested.

The words barely left his mouth when they heard the roar of water.

"Get out of the river!" Split the Waves yelled. "It's the ice dam! It's gone! Paddle or we'll all die!"

Split the Waves paddled furiously as a wall of water rushed down the valley. He leapt from his dug-out, dragging the boat with him as the waters snatched at his feet. His companions did not make it to shore.

"No! No!" he yelled, watching the furious wave hit Kretch and toss him and his boat like paper in a hurricane. They were soon lost in the fury of the river. Then he spotted Salkusta farther downriver trying to reach the shore.

"Salkusta, paddle! PADDLE!" he yelled at his friend.

Salkusta tried to race the water and keep afloat, but like an enormous tidal wave, the water raced towards him. The wall of water hit his dug-out, flipping him over in the turbulence. Split the Waves watched in horror as his friend was tossed in the angry waves and spun about with the trees and debris carried by the floodwaters. In seconds, Salkusta disappeared from sight.

It was some time before the water subsided. Split the Waves sat on the cliffs above the river, stunned by the catastrophe. As soon as it was safe to paddle, Split the Waves got into his boat and began searching for his friends. Washed up on the side of the river, he found a bundle of furs that Kretch had stowed in his boat, and then Split the Waves spotted a boat bobbing up in an eddy. A short distance downstream, he found his friend's body face down in an eddy, caught in the branches of an uprooted tree.

Split the Waves pulled Kretch to shore, held him in his arms and wailed in sorrow. Then he knelt over his friend and sang a prayer. He placed Kretch in the dug-out and towed him downstream continuing to search along the shore for Salkusta.

Surely he is also lost, he thought. *How could anyone survive the force of that flood of water?*

Split the Waves became too weary and dispirited to continue. He found a grassy hill along the river and pulled the boat with Kretch's body up the incline. There he prepared for his friend's burial, singing songs to send Kretch's spirit peacefully into the next life. Finally, Split the Waves placed dry wood about the boat and lit the funeral pyre. He sang the songs for the dead, his sad mournful voice ringing through the valley. Later, despite his exhaustion, sleep eluded him. All he could think of was how foolish he had been to ignore his grandmother's warning.

The sun dipped below the horizon as Split the Waves sat watching the river and brooding over the fate of his companions. Then, in the half-light of the midnight sun, he resumed his search for Salkusta, walking along the bank, fearful of what he might find.

"What is this?" Split the Waves said in surprise as he noticed a bright splash of colour on the edge of the shallow eddy below the cliff.

Split the Waves ran down to the river. A young girl lay on the shore. Her eyes were closed, but she was still breathing.

Julianna moaned as Split the Waves pulled her onto a dry spot on the bank.

"What?" Julianna gasped. "Who are you?"

"I–I call–called," he stuttered, not knowing what to say to this strange girl.

"What's your name?" Julianna was able to focus her eyes on her rescuer.

"I–I am called Kajach-hat. It means 'Split the Waves' in your English," he managed to say. "And what is your name?"

"I don't know. I–I can't remember." Julianna looked at the strange boy dressed in skins. He had dark eyes and was slim and muscular.

"Your clothes are weird," she said.

"My grandma made these for me. Maybe when I go to Skagway, I will trade them for the white man's trousers and shirt. What about your clothes? I have never seen a funny jacket like this before," he said, pointing to her purple lifejacket. "And this hat, it is hard like rock." He touched her helmet and ran his fingers over the dent. "You must be cold. Take off the wet clothing and I will give you some skins to wear. We have to get you warmed up. If you do not remember your name, I will have to name you. Maybe you be Hin-Shawot. That means 'River Woman' because I–I find you in the river. Is that okay?"

"Yes, I guess that will do," Julianna answered, feeling as if she had been dropped on another planet with her brain cells erased.

"Can you stand up and walk now, or maybe I help you?" He held her arm as she staggered to her feet. For a moment she felt dizzy and had to lean on Split the Waves for support. Gradually, her vision cleared and with Split the Waves by her side, she climbed up the bank.

"Here, put these on while I go get some firewood. I won't look at you." Split the Waves handed Julianna a bundle that included skin clothing and moccasins and disappeared into the woods. When he returned, she had finished changing.

"Now you look like a good Tlingit woman. Before, you looked like someone from another country with that strange hat. I never saw a hat like that before. But it must have saved your poor head from being smashed."

"You are like someone from another world, or maybe my head is so mixed up I don't remember anything. Where are we and where do you come from?"

"We are on the Alsek River. I stay with my grandma at Alsek and sometimes with my uncle at Klukwan. There was a big flood yesterday and all the water came out of the lake, with icebergs breaking loose. My friends were lost in the water." Split the Waves lowered his head and sat quietly looking out at the swollen river.

"I found Kretch and buried him on the river," he continued. "I did not find Salkusta."

"Who are they? Kre…I'm sorry, I can't pronounce their names."

"Kretch is called 'Hawk' in your language and Salkusta means 'Chipmunk.' They are my friends and go with me down the Alsek to trade with the Chilkats. Now maybe Salkusta is also dead. I do not know. It–it–it it is my fault. I did not listen to my grandma and they have paid with their lives."

Split the Waves was silent for a minute, then, concerned about Julianna, he continued. "Here, you better eat now because the cold water took all your strength." Split the Waves had cooked some moose meat brought from his village. He took the meat off a stick and tore off a portion for Julianna. She thanked him and gobbled the meat noisily. Split the Waves smiled at the sight of this strange girl.

"And do you come from across the water in the big ships?" Split the Waves asked as he slowly chewed his food.

"I can't remember," Julianna replied, with her mouth full. "I don't think I've been in an ocean-going ship. But I think I've been in a canoe and a raft before."

"Maybe you come from Dyea or Skagway where there are more and more of your people all the time. Now there is a new town of white people. Maybe you come from there. That is the place where water runs through steep canyon rocks. I went there to trade when the first snow fell last year and I saw maybe a few white traders. That is all. I went on a trail and then I built a boat that took me to Kwanlin Dun, or what the traders call 'White Horse' because the waves are like white horses. That is where I got my name, Split the Waves, because I went through the big water with my boat and everyone thought I would drown but instead my boat cut through the big waves. My grandpa was with me and named me that day."

"Everything you say is so strange. I seem to remember that I was with my school friends, but my memory is so faint that I can't recall them or my family or where I live," Julianna said.

"I do not go to school now because I am a trader. But when I was young the missionaries took me to Fort Selkirk where I learned to speak English and to even write in your language. It was hard because I had the stutter very bad then. Now it is mostly gone and I speak pretty good. What do you think?"

"You speak very well," Julianna said smiling, "and don't worry about your stutter. Did you say you went to school at Fort Selkirk? That place sounds familiar and so does Whitehorse. But I'm not sure."

"I went to Fort Selkirk when I was nine years old and they taught me about your Queen Victoria who is a great ruler across the ocean.

Do you know her?"

Julianna paused before replying. "Queen Victoria? Yes, I've heard of her. But what did you say about the date? What year is it? I can't even remember that."

"This year is 1898. I know that because the traders tell me. Only two years ago there was a big gold discovery in Trondek and lots of your people are crazy to come to our land now. Soon, all will change."

Julianna couldn't finish her supper. She left the campfire and wandered along the bank trying to find something that would help her remember her past. Then, she saw his boat. It wasn't a kayak or a canoe. It was a hand-carved dug-out. She reached into the boat and pulled out a bundle of furs.

"Oh, what has happened to me? Where am I?" Julianna's eyes filled with tears.

"I think you bumped your head on the canyon and forget who you are." Split the Waves had followed Julianna and saw she was crying. He spoke gently. "You will be okay with me. We will go down the Alsek to the Tatshenshini River and then we will trade the furs. We will see many white men, and they will know where your family is. Anyway, it is good I find you because I need you to paddle a boat and carry the furs from Kretch's boat. You paddle okay?" he asked.

"I'm pretty sure I can paddle, but I don't know if I could handle your boat. I sort of remember having a canoe or kayak but it didn't look like yours. But it doesn't matter because I don't have a boat."

"I will make one for you. It will only take a day, then we will paddle the river for three days down to the big water where we trade."

"How do you come back with all your trade goods? You can't go up the river."

"We will go to the Dyea River and pack over the Chilkoot Trail across the mountains. I've gone many times this way. We will go together and you can help me pack the blankets and pots and I will help you find your people. Is that good?" As he felt more comfortable with Julianna, he stuttered less.

The next day, Split the Waves made a small cut with his axe in a fir tree. He lit a fire in the tree so it would burn through, eventually bringing the tree down. His next job was hollowing out the tree to make a narrow boat for Julianna.

"While I make the boat, maybe you can get us a fish. There are grayling that taste good. You can take my spear from the boat."

Julianna did not want to admit that she had never even caught a fish with a hook. She picked up the spear and climbed down the cliff to a pool. She could see the fish resting in the quiet water but each time she threw the spear, the fish darted off. Julianna took her moccasins off and waded into the pool. Standing very quietly she waited until a grayling lay directly under the spear. She pierced the fish and brought it out of the water with a triumphant yell.

"Good work," Split the Waves congratulated her as she displayed her fish. "Do you remember how a fish is cooked, or has that memory gone too?" Split the Waves kidded her.

"I'll try," Julianna said, wondering just how she should clean and prepare the fish.

The boat was almost finished when Julianna called him for supper. Split the Waves looked at the fish and grinned.

"Maybe you have never learned to cut fish or to keep it from burning. Don't you have an auntie to teach you these things?" Split the Waves asked.

Julianna looked at the ragged pieces of burnt fish and blushed. "I've never had to clean and fillet a fish before. Sorry." She divided the fish up and served the meal on clean, flat rocks.

"I will pick out the burnt parts and then it tastes very good," Split the Waves said, concerned that his blunt comments about her cooking had hurt her feelings.

"I guess you have to teach me how to cook over a fire," Julianna replied. "Will the boat be ready soon?"

"Tomorrow we go down the river and maybe it will be difficult to keep from flipping. Do you know how to roll the boat up if it flips?" Split the Waves asked.

"You won't be able to roll this boat. There's no skirt!" Julianna exclaimed.

"A skirt. What you mean?"

"I think my boat had some kind of cover that kept the water from coming into my boat. Then, when I rolled the boat I stayed dry. If I tried to roll your dug-out, the water would keep me from coming up and I would have to swim," Julianna explained.

"I never swim. It does not matter that the boat is full of water, I still bring it up, then I paddle to the shore and pour the water out." Split the Waves offered this as factual information, not in a boasting manner.

"But that is no good because you always have to stop and empty your boat. Why don't we make skirts for the boats and then I will be safe and you won't have to pour water from your boat?"

"How you do this?"

"Let's use two of your skins, and we'll make a skirt that fits around our waists and is attached to the boat. Here, I'll show you."

Julianna cut the skins and with a needle borrowed from Split the Waves, she sewed the skirts. Her stitching was clumsy, but the pieces held together well enough to work. Before bedtime she had two skirts made, and Split the Waves had her boat finished. That night they placed strips of fish on a rack to smoke and dry overnight so they would have food for their journey.

The next morning, Julianna slipped into the dug-out and tried to roll in the awkward boat. She was close to shore, attempting her roll in the shallow pond. Julianna purposely flipped the boat, swept the paddle through the water, came part-way up, and flipped under again. She tried a second time, gasping for air as her face came out of the water. She couldn't bring the boat up with the short paddle. This time Split the Waves helped her so she wouldn't get wet.

"I will show you how to use these paddles, okay?"

Split the Waves flipped the boat and came up smiling. "I like this skirt you made me. I do not even get wet now."

Julianna watched the sweep of his paddle and concentrated on imitating his roll. She flipped, swept the small paddle back and brought the boat upright.

"I think we're ready," Julianna said. "If there are big rapids, I'll just roll up on the next wave."

"Downriver there is a big mixing of the rivers and lots of waves, but now we will both be okay," Split the Waves smiled.

CHAPTER 5

PADDLE TO THE SEA

Julianna and Split the Waves paddled into the river on a gloriously sunny spring day. Although Julianna worried from time to time about her loss of memory, she could not help but enjoy the trip. She could talk to Split the Waves about anything without having to be embarrassed; she didn't have to pretend that she hated him; and she actually could admit to herself that she liked being with this strange young man.

Split the Waves named the birds, the trees and the fish in Tlingit, and Julianna would try and remember what they were called in English.

"Do you smell the ocean now? Just a bit of the sea comes up the valley to meet us," Split the Waves said, sniffing the air like an animal.

"We're a long way from the ocean," Julianna replied. "We haven't even reached the Tatshenshini River and then we have to pass the glacier and through Lake Alsek with the icebergs…and then I'll be able to smell the ocean."

"How come you know the river almost as much as me? Have you been down trading many times?"

"No, I don't know anything about trading. I haven't been on this river before, but I have been told about it and I sort of remember going down the Tatshenshini. I think I was travelling with friends on the Alsek River, and I know that we'll join the Tatshenshini River and then reach the ocean." Julianna was pleased that a few memories remained.

He sniffed the air again. "Mmm, I sure like the smell of the ocean."

"You're different. Maybe you can smell and hear more than me because you are part animal, like a wolf."

"They called me wolf pup when I was young because I cried a lot. I was very unhappy, because my mother and father died when I was only four years old. I had trouble to talk and only stuttered."

"I know this is strange, but I seem to remember having a childhood friend who stuttered."

"I hope you will find your people, and that I will find Salkusta. I am worried that he has been taken by the river like Kretch."

"I know you've been looking for Salkusta, but it is probably hopeless for anyone to have survived that flood of water."

"Salkusta is very strong. He would not give up to the water. If anyone would ride the water, it would be Salkusta," Split the Waves claimed. "And now we will see how your boat behaves in the big waves," he remarked, looking downstream at the churning waters.

"Stay near me, Split the Waves. I'm not sure I can make it."

"I will watch for you all the way. We will meet at the bottom in the big eddy."

The two boats plunged into the fury of the river. Powerful currents met in the middle of the river and pushed waves high into the air. The small boats were tossed on the surging water, were dipped into the hollows between the waves, and rose up on the crest. Julianna kept her craft speeding forward, continually correcting the boat whenever the waves began to flip her.

Suddenly, a towering wave rose up ahead, as high as a house. With all her strength, she drove forward into the water, hoping she had enough power to ride over the wave. The small boat climbed the wave. She was almost at the top of the wave when a cross-current hit her, flipping the boat over. Julianna held her breath and waited. If she tried to roll up too early, she would still be in the midst of the foamy water with nothing for her paddle to grip onto. Now! She reached up with the short paddle and, thinking through each phase of the sweep, she brought the boat upright.

"Wow! I made it!" Julianna yelled triumphantly as she paddled towards Split the Waves.

But he did not reply. He was on the gravel beach bending over something. Julianna paddled into the eddy where a dug-out floated near the shore.

"Is it Salkusta?" she asked.

"Yes, and he is alive but in pain. Come and help me."

A young native man lay curled up on the sand, holding his shoulder and grimacing in pain.

Split the Waves spoke to his friend in Tlingit and then turned to Julianna.

"His shoulder is out. Look how his arm is hanging," Split the Waves said. "He did this before, and it took so much pain to get the arm back in its place. I think you have some medicine in the pocket of your funny jacket?"

"It's a lifejacket," Julianna replied. "But I don't remember having any medicine."

"Here, I will get it for you," Split the Waves said, reaching into the large pocket at the back of Julianna's lifejacket and pulling out a first-aid kit. "See, lots of medicine and bandages."

Julianna removed a small waterproof case, checked the label and took out three pills. Salkusta was moaning in pain. "Can you swallow these?" she asked gently.

Salkusta looked at Split the Waves with a puzzled expression.

Split the Waves explained what was happening in their native language, and Salkusta opened his mouth to accept the pills. In a few minutes, he seemed to be more comfortable and smiled sleepily from the effects of the strong pain relievers.

"Salkusta, we have to put your shoulder back in and maybe it will hurt," Split the Waves said.

"I am ready for it this time because of good medicine," Salkusta replied.

"River Woman, can you lift his arm up straight and I will try and push it into place?"

Split the Waves pushed firmly on the head of the bone, trying to get it into the socket. Salkusta clenched his teeth as Split the Waves put more pressure on the bone. There was a clunking sound as the bone slipped into the socket.

"Hey, we did it!" Split the Waves smiled.

"Now I will make a comfortable sling for your arm and soon you will be as good as new." Split the Waves repeated Julianna's words in Tlingit to make sure Salkusta understood. Julianna took a piece of folded cotton cloth from her first-aid supplies and carefully lifted Salkusta's arm into the sling. Salkusta grinned at Julianna as she fussed over him.

"There, now you'll be comfortable. Rest while I bring you some tea," she said.

"You good woman. I marry you but I already promised to a Han princess," Salkusta said with a broad smile.

"That's okay, I'm too young to marry," Julianna replied.

"I don't think you too young. She must be thirteen years, don't you think so, Split the Waves?"

"I am fourteen," Julianna said.

"Hey, that is almost old woman. We will have to find you a husband," Salkusta continued. "Maybe Split the Waves should marry you. He is rich man already."

Julianna blushed at Salkusta's friendly chiding.

Split the Waves helped Julianna with the fire, and in a few minutes she returned with a cup of hot sweetened tea.

"Drink it slowly," she cautioned.

Salkusta accepted the tea with a smile that spread over his round face. He lifted the tea to his lips and gulped down the sugary drink.

"Slowly, Salkusta," she cautioned.

"Slo—what that?" he smiled, handing the cup back to Julianna. "More."

Split the Waves replied to Salkusta in Tlingit and then repeated in English, "Slowly means you do this." Split the Waves took small sips from his tea.

"Now that we have River Woman with us, we will learn the English better and be ready to trade with the Americans when we reach the ocean," Split the Waves suggested.

"I speak the English," Salkusta protested. "Not all English, a part."

Julianna laughed, "I will teach you English, Salkusta, if you will teach me Tlingit."

CHAPTER 6

THE HUNT

The three new friends ate a big breakfast of meat, berries and bannock and sat around the campfire until noon before loading the boats. Salkusta's shoulder was still sore, forcing him to use only one arm to pack his boat.

"I told you that Salkusta holds onto his boat," Split the Waves remarked as he helped his friend load supplies.

"It is only way I could stay above the water, to hold onto the boat. That is how me shoulder came out," Salkusta explained.

When they were ready, Julianna pushed him off from the shore.

"It's easy water," Split the Waves said, "only a few waves but not so that the entire river is dangerous."

"Just enjoy the sunshine and stay in the quiet water," Julianna added.

That day the water was calm, almost too flat for Julianna who yearned for waves and excitement. After several hours of flat water paddling, she moved her boat close to the bank to catch the wave action. Split the Waves followed her, admiring Julianna's spunk. Salkusta stayed out in the middle of the river, floating gently downstream to avoid using his injured arm.

Julianna spotted waves on the far side of the river and paddled hard to reach the white water that piled up along a steep cliff. Split the Waves watched as his new friend sped over to the waves. Then he realized that she was heading for danger, where the river poured along both sides of a small, rocky island. Julianna had thought the waves were caused by the cliffs along the shore, and had unwittingly paddled into the dangerous watershed on the upstream side of the island. It was too late to warn Julianna. Her small boat lodged on the cliff of the island, pinned by the force of the water that piled on the mid-river island.

"Help! Help!" Julianna screamed, remembering that many kayakers died when their boats were pinned against a cliff by the force of the water.

Split the Waves spun his dug-out over to the island. Julianna's head was barely above the waves, and her boat was filling with water.

Oh my God! I'm going under! She felt herself being sucked below the waves. The water was level with her neck, when, with a surge of strength, she pushed out of the boat, freeing herself from the entrapment. Julianna gasped as she was tossed in the waves, bouncing along the side of the cliff. It was all she could do to save herself.

As she bobbed through the waves, Split the Waves caught up to her. "Hold onto my boat and I will tow you to shore."

Julianna passed her paddle to Split the Waves, then grabbed onto his boat with one hand and reached out to hold her boat with the other.

Split the Waves towed her to a gravel beach. Salkusta pulled his boat into shore with a grin on his face. "You play and get into big trouble."

Julianna felt ashamed. "You're right, and I feel a bit foolish." She thought, *I don't know why I do things like that. I always tell myself to be careful and then when there is no good reason, I put myself and others in danger. One of these days I will grow up!*

"You are a pretty smart girl all right, but brave like a warrior or maybe one who fights the grizzly bear," Split the Waves replied. "That is good. I think I like a woman like that. What you think, Salkusta? Your sweetie from Trondek is not like that, is she?"

"No, she never goes in the rapids. She mostly walks. When she stays with her auntie, she sews such beautiful things that when we marry I will be best-dressed man in village. She even speaks the English good like Split the Waves because the priest opened a school for her village."

"And when the big wedding happens, do we get to come to a potlatch at Trondek and eat and dance for a week?"

"It will be the greatest potlatch. The people will come together and we celebrate. She has wealthy families among the Tlingit and the Trondek."

"She is like a princess if she was English," Split the Waves explained.

"Salkusta's bride is from two great families of leaders. Not only is she from important families but she is very beautiful and knows all the ways of making food and clothing." Split the Waves smiled. "I think she will have a pretty fine husband, too."

"If I make much money trading, I will buy her many presents when we are at Dyea."

"Time for us to sleep now. Salkusta will dream of Katu, and maybe I will dream about my new English friend."

"And maybe I will dream about beautiful big waves in the river so I am not foolish again and put myself and others in danger," Julianna added as she put out her bedroll beside the fire.

They talked quietly as the setting sun cast gold and red rays across the mountain peaks. There was a short night before the first rays of sunlight signalled the beginning of a new day. Despite the early sunrise, Julianna slept until Split the Waves woke her.

"I have tea for you and bannock will be ready soon."

Julianna jumped up. "I'm sorry I was not up to help. You must think I am lazy, just waiting for everyone to feed me. I will make the supper tonight and you will rest."

"First, we paddle more rapids. Once I flipped in this rapid and had a big swim. Today is a problem because Salkusta must not paddle with his injured arm," Split the Waves said with concern.

"Why not make a boat big enough for three people and all the furs and our gear?"

"They make big boats where we go to the village on this river and my grandfather made big boats for the Yukon River."

"If you pick out the right tree, I'll help you."

"That will be good. We do this together like cousins, okay?"

They found a large fir tree and lit a fire that would burn into the trunk at the foot of the tree. The boat builders remained by the tree to tend the fire and see that it did not spread.

"I like finding ways of avoiding hard work. If we had tried to cut this tree down, we would be wearing ourselves out and our axes," Julianna remarked as she watched the flames eat into the bottom of the tree. Soon, it had burned half-way through the trunk. They doused the fire and with a few blows Split the Waves felled the tree. They lit another fire under the tree to burn out the hollow. Finally, it was time to carve the boat.

Salkusta and Split the Waves had axes, and Julianna took her knife from her lifejacket, anxious to help on the project. However, the task was difficult and tiring. The tree was huge and their tools were small. Little by little they hacked away at the tree, gradually increasing the hollow. They worked for two days to complete the task.

When the canoe was ready, they decided to take an extra day to hunt so they would have fresh meat for the journey. Salkusta had no problem with the hike up the mountain. They left the willows and aspen of the valley and moved above the treeline into the alpine area. Below, they could see the braided river, like silver threads stretching through the valley, joining and parting again. Above them were the glaciated Coastal Mountains. The sun was bright, but as they climbed the mountain, a cool wind blew away the bugs and turned the hunting trip into a party.

"Quiet," Salkusta whispered, pointing to a herd of mountain goats on a cliff above them. "Split the Waves and me, we go downwind of them. You," motioning to Julianna, "break off some willows and wave them at the herd so they run to us."

The two young men crept along the rocky face, making their way to the far side of the herd. Split the Waves had the bow, and Salkusta held the arrows.

Julianna cut two or three willow branches in a ravine on the mountain side. She wanted to hurry lest the herd move on, but she had to be careful not to make a sound. She was excited to be part of the hunt.

Julianna made her way slowly towards the herd. As she poked her head over the rocks, one of the goats looked back at her as if he knew she was there all the time. Julianna stood up and waved the branches, and the goats fled up the mountain. Julianna waited excitedly, not knowing whether the hunt would be successful.

"Come help us!" Split the Waves called from across the bluff. Julianna ran over to find Split the Waves skinning the goat, with Salkusta helping. "Here, pull on the hide while I cut. This will make a good sale to the traders so I don't want to ruin it with a knife cut."

Julianna was fascinated watching Split the Waves skin, gut and cut up the animal, and kept asking him, "What is this part?" "What is that part?" "Is it a male or female?"

"Haven't you ever seen a dead animal before?" Split the Waves asked, smiling at Julianna. "The little children in the village know more than you about the animals."

"I know I am pretty dumb, but I don't think I've ever hunted before."

"Don't your dad or uncle hunt for the meat?" Salkusta looked puzzled.

"I don't think so."

"I don't think I like the way you live," Salkusta continued. "You should stay here with us where life is much better. We will get you a grandma to teach you to cut up the animals and gut fish and dry meat and salmon. Make a good Tlingit woman out of you," he said with a friendly chuckle. "What you think, Split the Waves? Would anyone marry a woman who cannot cut the meat or sew clothes?"

Julianna understood he was joking and took the teasing with a big smile.

"And what about you, Salkusta," Split the Waves retaliated. "Now that you have a broken wing, River Woman will have to paddle you to the ocean and you will sit like an old woman in the boat, and she will carry more meat than you when we go down."

"I will take my load," Salkusta said, "as long as we have some food before we hike. I like it up here without the bugs and with the mountains keeping watch above us."

The group made tea and ate leftover bannock. They roasted some of the meat over the fire and then rested. Julianna couldn't have felt happier. The two young men looked at each other and grinned as they watched Julianna wolf down her food.

"You different," Salkusta said. "In our village, young women must always eat with small bites. You eat like hungry bear. Who in your village teach you to eat like that?"

"I remember going on a long canoe trip with this really funny leader," Julianna replied. "He taught me to eat my food as fast as possible so I would fool my stomach into believing I was still hungry. That way, we would eat more and be strong paddlers." Julianna was pleased that one or two memories remained.

"Our girls go to stay with their grandma or auntie when they are just becoming women. They learn to serve the Elders first and then eat slowly after everyone else has been fed. But we like the way you eat. Maybe we should call you Hungry Bear as well as River Woman," Split the Waves laughed.

The next day they finished the boat and packed for the journey to the ocean. They spent their last night at the camp, talking late into the night. Split the Waves told of his days at school when he was taken to Fort Selkirk by the missionaries.

"I was there several years, learning to speak the English. We sat in hard desks and slept in cold buildings. When I spoke my language to a cousin, I was beaten. Some of the people were good to us, but it was not for me. I ran away as soon as I was old enough to travel on my own."

"But you must have been very young. How did you ever get home? Fort Selkirk is a long way from your village."

"Hey, that is no problem for us. We have relatives along the Yukon River and we know the trails. I was lucky because the weather stayed mild and I had stolen enough food to keep me from starving."

"Did you hunt for food?" Julianna asked, thinking of how easily he had found their food on this trip.

"Sure I hunted, but all I got was a gopher. I had lots to learn about hunting, and I did not have any arrow heads and no tools, only a little string to make snares. Anyway, I lived. My other friend, he died trying to get back home."

"That is why my mother and father not let them take me," Salkusta said. "They know many children run away and die before they reach home. Instead, my mother and father teach me." Salkusta had the comfortable assurance of one who had always been loved, protected and cared for.

"When I was maybe only four years, I stayed with m–m–," Split the Waves stuttered as he remembered his painful childhood, "my…uncle and aunt. We did not get along so they gave me up to the English. After I ran off, I stayed with my grandfather at Kwanlin and he taught me to become a man. Everything I know of hunting and going through the big water, I learned from my grandfather."

The next day, the Alsek River joined the beautiful Tatshenshini, the river that was home to the salmon. Here the valley broadened out, and it was difficult to choose the route with the fastest water. Soon after the confluence, they would reach the turbulent area of the river where water came from several channels and pushed up into diagonal waves, boils and cross-currents.

When they entered the rapids, Julianna paddled in the bow and called out the direction. As the craft lifted into the air, Julianna leaned forward and braced hard against her paddle. The back of the boat submerged in the foam and for a few minutes they thought the boat would flip. But they surfaced and pushed against the foaming water, sending the canoe forward and out of the diagonal waves.

Salkusta's fate was in the hands of the paddlers. Julianna and Split the Waves paddled well together. Both had the ability to react instantaneously to the huge waves, bracing as the boat tilted to one side or the other, steering the craft directly into the current if it began to veer to the side, powering through the forward surges of water, and slowing the boat down as they moved up a gigantic wave.

There was a set of rollers, and then the boat slipped into the quiet waters. Julianna was so exhilarated she felt like hugging her companions. "Wow, that was great. I loved it! Did you like that, Salkusta? Wasn't that awesome, Split the Waves?"

There was no answer.

"Hey, are you two still there?" Julianna asked, looking back at her companions. "Why are you so quiet?"

"We do not say much about the big water, because next time the water may take us. It is out of respect," Salkusta answered.

"I liked it too, but Salkusta is right," Split the Waves added. "We have to be careful not to say words that make it seem like we were the ones to make the trip safely. It is not just us. It is also those that care for us and sing the songs to keep us safe."

Julianna understood what her companions were saying. She could recall parts of her past and remembered that good kayakers never whooped and hollered after running a difficult set of rapids. Now it was made clear to Julianna that was the Tlingit way as well.

After the set of rapids, the water was slow and winds came up the valley, pushing against their little boat. They were hoping to camp near the big glacier and worked hard to move the boat faster. Julianna strained on the paddle, barely able to continue. Then the glacier came into sight. A long tongue of blue and black ice curled down from the mountain side, leaving only a ribbon of sandy dunes and clumps of willows between the ice and the water.

"There it is!" Julianna exclaimed, happy to know that their campsite was in view. "If this wind would just stop, we'd be there in a flash."

"What you say?" Salkusta yelled back.

But their words were lost in the roar of the wind. The gale was so strong that they were unable to move the boat forward. Suddenly the wind gusted, and the boat turned sideways to the current and began to tip.

"Yi!" Salkusta yelled, feeling helpless and trying hard not to grab onto the gunnels. Water sloshed over the side, dousing Salkusta, who crouched low in the centre of the boat. Julianna didn't care if she was soaked, but worried about flipping in the middle of the wide river because Salkusta would never make it to shore with only one arm. Julianna leaned downstream and planted a strong high brace, trying to bring the boat upright. Water filled the craft to the rim. Split the Waves was now submerged in water. Salkusta tumbled out of the upstream side of the boat, and over they went—paddlers, boat and the supplies that had not been tied in.

Julianna gasped as she sank in the icy water. Her first thought was to find Salkusta. She pushed up to the surface and gripped the tip of the canoe. Split the Waves and Salkusta were not in sight! All she could see were pieces of gear pushed about in the wind.

"Oh please, help!" Julianna called out desperately. She could not understand how such flat water could take Split the Waves and Salkusta, who had survived the wall of water when the ice dam burst. *It couldn't be!*

Julianna dove under but could see nothing in the silt-laden, glacial waters. She surfaced for a breath and pushed herself under the canoe. She could not see but reached out and felt a limp body and a tangle of ropes. She was running out of air.

Julianna surfaced and gasped for air, then saw Split the Waves come up for a breath. He held a knife in his hand. Julianna realized that Salkusta was caught under the boat. She pulled out her knife and sunk down, cutting the ropes that tangled about Salkusta. Then Split the Waves and Julianna pulled their friend to the surface.

Panting from a lack of air, she grabbed onto the canoe with one hand and both she and Split the Waves held Salkusta's limp head out of the water. He wasn't breathing.

"Hold him!" Julianna slid forward on the upturned canoe, gripping the boat with her legs to free her arms. She tilted Salkusta's head back, pinched his nose and breathed into his mouth.

"I feel his pulse. His heart is beating. Keep the air going!" Split the Waves said urgently, as he held onto the canoe with one hand and propped Salkusta's head out of the water with the other.

How many minutes can you live without air? Julianna wondered, as she kept up the rhythmic breathing. It seemed like forever that he had been under the water, and now he was still without oxygen.

"Do not stop. He is only under the water for a couple of minutes," Split the Waves said, encouraging Julianna. "He will make it, I know."

Julianna said nothing but gained hope from Split the Waves' words. She could keep this up for hours if she thought it would save Salkusta. She breathed hard into his lungs and saw the air fill his chest. Then Salkusta coughed violently, spewing out water.

"Quick, lean him over the canoe," Split the Waves yelled. They both worked to flip Salkusta onto his stomach where he continued coughing and spitting out water.

"River Woman, get to other side of boat and hold Salkusta's hands so he won't slip off."

Julianna understood. She grasped Salkusta firmly and spoke to him reassuringly. "You'll be okay, Salkusta. We'll get you to shore. I'll hold you on the boat and we'll make it. That's it, just get all that water out of your stomach." The sling had come loose and Salkusta winced in pain when Julianna grasped his hands to hold him over the bottom of the dug-out.

"Hey, Split the Waves! What are you doing?" She was surprised to see him crawl onto the end of the upturned canoe and begin paddling them towards shore.

As if in sympathy with their plight, the wind suddenly died down. Now it was relatively easy to move the boat with the current. As they slipped through the water, Split the Waves reached down to pick up flotsam. He retrieved a bundle of furs, bags that held their supplies, and the sack of food. He threw the fur robes over the upturned boat. The other things kept slipping off the boat, so he held several of them in his teeth.

Salkusta stopped coughing and managed a faint smile.

Julianna smiled back. "That's better, Salkusta. I knew you would make it." She looked back to see Split the Waves with ropes hanging from his mouth.

"You look like a monster, Split the Waves," Julianna laughed.

Salkusta continued coughing.

"Coughin goo fer hm…," Split the Waves tried to talk with all the gear clamped in his teeth.

Julianna imitated him. "Was ath yoo say?" she laughed again and Salkusta, seeing Split the Waves with ropes hanging from his mouth, started laughing. This mirth set off another series of coughs.

"Hey, I can touch the bottom. It's shallow enough to walk!" Julianna exclaimed, standing up in the quiet water.

Split the Waves jumped off the boat and speaking to Salkusta in Tlingit, asked if he could stand on his own for a minute while the boat was righted.

Salkusta tried to stand up and staggered a bit. "Here, steady yourself with the paddle," Split the Waves said. "Okay, you ready? We will pour the water out first."

Split the Waves tipped the canoe up slightly until it broke the seal with the surface of the water.

"Are you strong enough to lift the canoe with so much stuff inside?" he asked.

"Do you think white women are weaklings?" Julianna replied, lifting her end of the canoe.

Split the Waves had to work fast to keep up with her. "Hey, wait for me to lift, River Woman, remember I am just a young man, not big and fat yet."

Some gear was tied to the struts of the canoe, making the load very heavy. Julianna was anxious to prove her strength and pushed the heavy load up and over her head. Water poured out and gear hung from ropes. They held the boat up while the water drained out.

"Okay, let it down." Julianna was happy to comply.

They helped Salkusta get into the dug-out. Before climbing in themselves, they retrieved the gear that Split the Waves had been carrying, and rescued other items that floated in the eddy. Soon, they were sending the craft swiftly to the shore.

It was a cool evening with a clear sky. The sun had just dipped below the mountain peak to the west. Julianna shivered as they beached the canoe and rushed about to find dry firewood. Salkusta was able to move about slowly but was obviously affected by the ordeal. His lips were blue from the lack of oxygen and the cold water.

"Matches! They'll all be wet!" Julianna shouted to Split the Waves who was pulling dry witches' broom from a spruce tree.

"We will start the fire with my flint," Split the Waves answered. He was carefully arranging the twigs in a fire pit.

Split the Waves dug through the packs and took out his flint. Soon he had a fire going. Julianna helped Salkusta remove his wet clothing and found a sheltered spot for him next to the fire.

"Here are some dry furs," Julianna announced as she removed the robes from a watertight bag made of an animal stomach. "Wrap this around yourself, Salkusta. And we'd better change, too," Julianna said to Split the Waves.

Split the Waves built a lean-to behind the fire and placed spruce branches on the ground. The three young people, wrapped in cozy furs, sat about the fire enjoying the heat. Salkusta recovered quickly and was ready to share the meal of roasted goat meat.

Their camp was on a sandbar near the glacier. After supper, Julianna and Split the Waves built a sauna. They dug into the sand and constructed a frame of willows that they covered with the wet skins. Salkusta rested and watched as his companions heated rocks and rolled them into the sauna. They found small skin garments in their bags and entered the steamy sauna. Salkusta joined them, enjoying the warmth after his icy dip.

Julianna sat next to Split the Waves, not embarrassed at being so close to her scantily clad friend. When Julianna and Split the Waves became too warm, they dashed out, dipped in the icy river and ran back to the warmth of the sauna. The heat was good for Salkusta's injured arm. It also relaxed the three tired travellers. Soon they were sleepy and rolled out their robes around the fire for a sound rest.

The next day they paddled into a valley surrounded by snow-capped mountains. To the west they could see a high peak, crowned with ice and piercing the clouds. The weather improved as they floated into the lake and met with the dazzling icebergs. It was like a wonderland. There was no wind and the sun was bright. They floated on green water surrounded by enormous blue icebergs, some as high as a cathedral. Julianna was afraid one of the icebergs would tip over and submerge them and wanted to stay far away from the immense forms. Split the Waves, who had been through the lake many times, also kept a safe distance from the larger icebergs. He was less concerned about the smaller bergs. He landed the canoe near one of the little floating ice islands, jumped nimbly from the canoe onto the floating iceberg and danced to entertain his companions.

"I think we should leave you here. You look like you could paddle that iceberg to the ocean," Julianna laughed.

In response, Split the Waves pretended to paddle the iceberg, sitting on the top and moving his arms as if he held a paddle.

"Do you think we should take him back?" Julianna asked Salkusta.

"Me and you should go and camp, make good dinner so he smell the meat and let him starve on the iceberg," Salkusta answered, with a twinkle in his eyes.

"But who will paddle through the roller coaster downriver from the lake?" Julianna said, faintly remembering that she had been through those rapids once in the past.

"You can do okay alone, no?" Salkusta asked.

"Sorry, I think I need him. I guess he will have to come back in the canoe." Julianna paddled over to the iceberg, which had drifted across the river. "We thought it over and decided you should come back with us. Anyway, I am hungry and I don't see anywhere to camp. Just maybe, I need your help to get to shore before my tummy starts grumbling."

"I think your people never go hungry," Split the Waves remarked.

"You're right," Julianna replied. "I remember lots of food. All kinds of fruit and cans and cans of food—big stores filled with every type of food from all over the world."

"There is lots of food and strange new things the English bring in the big boats," Split the Waves said. "Soon you will see when we get to the ocean."

63

CHAPTER 7

THE TLINGIT VILLAGE

Soon the three travellers would reach the coastline where ships from across the ocean and the American coastal cities came to trade with the Tlingits. They would spend one night at the lake and if they paddled for a long day, they would reach the camp of the Tlingits who controlled trade on the Alsek. From there, Split the Waves would decide whether to walk over the trail to Klukwan, or go in the big ocean-going boats with his relatives. Klukwan was the birthplace of his grandmother. There, Split the Waves would be cared for and given the best opportunity to make a good trade.

It was a long walk by land and a dangerous journey by water. Split the Waves was quiet that night as he pondered the choices he would have to make once they reached the ocean.

When the river flattened out, Split the Waves began searching for a channel that would lead to the Tlingit village.

"It looks different," Split the Waves explained with a puzzled look. "When the ice dam went, I think the water came through and changed everything. The village had to be here, just over on that bank." They paddled across to the river's edge and walked up the bank. The longhouse was battered and abandoned. Debris was scattered about, swept across the land by the receding waters.

"Everyone is gone! The river took all the village," Split the Waves said, worried that loved ones may have been lost in the flood.

They camped a short distance from the village. Split the Waves spoke very little. All he could think of was the terror the people must have felt as the water roared towards them. He hoped they were able to escape and that he would still find his aunt and cousins.

"Now we can't go with my people by boat, but to carry all the furs over the trail is too heavy. We need an ocean boat," he said. "They used to have several boats in the village and my cousins would take us over the big water to Klukwan in just a day, maybe two."

"Maybe your people escaped in the boats. I think we find your people and row to Klukwan," Salkusta suggested.

"I can help you row," Julianna offered.

"I don't know about a woman rowing the ocean boats. The Tlingits don't bring their women, do they, Split the Waves? I was told that it brings bad luck to have a woman even touch the boat, especially if she is at that time of month. I never go against the rules," Salkusta said shaking his head.

"With me along, all rules will get broken," Julianna replied. "Just because I am white doesn't mean you can treat me without respect."

"It is not a matter of respect. There is always great respect for you," Salkusta replied. "It is the Tlingit way, and we don't go against those laws."

"You really mean that I won't be able to go in the boat with you? You must be kidding." Julianna's face was red.

"What you mean, kidding?" Split the Waves said nervously. He disliked any aggression and felt uncomfortable at the tone of Julianna's voice.

"What I mean, you male chauvinists, is that I can go in the boat, that if you don't let me in the boat our friendship is over." Julianna stomped over to the river and sat gazing out to the sea, fuming with anger. "I can't believe that they would even want to go without me. They need me to help paddle," she mumbled to herself.

A few minutes passed before Split the Waves walked over to Julianna.

"I am sorry you are unhappy. We come from such different places, that sometimes it is hard for us to understand you. We agree, you can come. We need more paddlers for the big boat," Split the Waves placed his hands on her shoulders and gave her a comforting squeeze. "Will you stop being angry with me now?" Split the Waves voice was kind.

"I was just hurt because I didn't think you appreciated me. Thank you for coming over. Most of the time I say things I don't really mean and then I'm sorry. You always take the first step to being friends again—something I will learn from you. Okay?"

"That is good, my friend. We will never have hard words again."

"Maybe there was no need to argue because we haven't found a boat yet, have we?" Julianna said.

While they paddled downriver they found tents, pots and clothing. They had almost given up hope of finding a boat, or signs of the Tlingit village, when they rounded a bend and were met by a welcome sight. Smoke curled up above the trees on the riverbank. They doubled the pace of their strokes and landed on shore where a group of Tlingit people welcomed them, calling out to Split the Waves and Salkusta with friendly smiles for the travellers.

A middle-aged woman, dressed in beautifully decorated skins, met Split the Waves and put her arms around him, crying as she spoke. Julianna couldn't understand what they were saying. Split the Waves turned to Julianna.

"This is my Auntie Hutlaun, but you can call her Jenny, her name from the English school," Split the Waves said to Julianna. "She tells me that most people were saved, but two fishermen were drowned. One was Jenny's cousin, the other, my uncle." Then he continued, "Auntie, this girl has lost her family and we look after her. She also lost her memory, even her name, so we call her River Woman."

Jenny smiled at Julianna. "Welcome to our camp. Many of our belongings were lost when the village upriver was flooded, but I will make sure you are well looked after."

"River Woman, when we are in camp there are certain rules to follow," Split the Waves said. "There are ways that we live with each other. I've asked Auntie if she would see that you learn how young women behave in our villages."

Julianna wanted to tell him that she did not care to have anyone teach her, but decided to check her tongue.

"That would be very kind of you," Julianna answered politely.

"Come with me, River Woman. I will bring you to my mother, who lives back of the camp," Jenny said. She led Julianna through the village. "Our people are still recovering from the flood, but we were fortunate that this village was spared."

Children ran beside them, staring at Julianna because of her blonde hair and blue eyes. Split the Waves and Salkusta were led to an old longhouse that had survived the flood.

Julianna was upset at being separated from her companions. When

Jenny noticed, she explained, "In our village the young girls are separated from others while they learn to become a woman. It also protects the hunters." The handsome woman spoke perfect English.

"Protect them from me? I am sorry but I don't understand." Julianna remained polite, although she was tempted once again to protest.

"I know it is difficult for a child raised with the white people. The Tlingits are very strict about young women. The Elders tell us if young women eat and stay in the camp with others, harm will come to the hunters on the mountains and boats will be lost in the sea."

"Split the Waves told me about this but I have to admit I don't really understand. What must I do?" Julianna asked, beginning to feel more comfortable with this well-spoken woman.

"You will be under the care of my mother. She doesn't speak your language so I will always be close by. There she is. When you meet her, call her Grandma. But that is all the English she will understand."

A wrinkled old woman sat on a log beside a brush hut. A blanket was wrapped about her and she wore skin clothing. Her face was very strange and frightening. The bottom lip protruded out almost two inches. It looked like a small saucer had been inserted in the old woman's lip. At first, Julianna couldn't help but stare. Then she realized she was being rude and looked away.

"It's a labret," Jenny said. "Women from the old days placed pieces of wood inside their lips as a sign of their rank in the tribe. My mother comes from a line of wealthy chiefs," Jenny explained.

"Oh, I see and I'm sorry for staring. That was very impolite of me." Julianna was still a little frightened at being placed under the care of this strange old person who could not even communicate with her.

Jenny spoke to her mother in Tlingit. The old woman nodded and then scowled at Julianna.

"I don't think she likes me," Julianna whispered to Jenny.

"She agreed to teach you, but told me she thinks the English girl won't learn well and won't be respectful."

"Please tell her that I will do all she tells me to do and that I appreciate she is willing to teach me." Julianna was pleased that she could swallow her pride and allow herself to be placed under the authority of this frightening old woman.

"I will leave for a short while now, and I will come to see you often in the next few weeks."

"Weeks! Surely I am not staying here that long! We have to go by boat to Klukwan and Dyea."

"The village won't let you go. It is not right. I hope you understand our ways," Jenny said, with some compassion as she realized how difficult it was for Julianna to be thrown into this foreign culture.

"The men will go with the boat along the coast and take your companions and their furs to trade. You and I will go by the trail and meet them. It will be all right. Don't worry, River Woman." With that, Julianna was left with the old grandmother.

Julianna managed a weak smile. The old woman scowled back and motioned Julianna to sit. The grandmother handed Julianna some beads, a needle and pieces of soft, tanned skin, and spoke to her in Tlingit. Julianna shook her head, indicating that she did not know how to sew. The grandmother muttered something that Julianna interpreted as "stupid girl," then began to show Julianna what to do with the skins. The old woman worked quickly and deftly, sewing the beads into a beautiful pattern.

Julianna watched carefully and began stringing the beads and sewing them on the pieces of skin. She could see that the sections were cut to make a moccasin. She sewed as carefully as she could but realized her work was not nearly as good as the grandmother's.

The old woman looked at the work, grabbed the skin and pulled out the stitches. Julianna felt the urge to walk away but resisted. *I must try harder*, she thought. She smiled at the old woman and put out her hand, indicating that she was willing to try again. This time the grandmother spoke kindly to Julianna and smiled back. The afternoon passed quickly and by the time Jenny arrived with supper, Julianna's stitches had improved considerably.

"Maybe this will be another disappointment," Jenny said, as she handed Julianna a bowl. "I hope you don't mind too much, but the young women cannot eat hot meat, only cold broth and bannock."

"Anything is welcome," Julianna said with a smile, "especially if it is someone else's cooking. Thank you." Julianna remembered Split the Waves' warning about eating habits and resisted gobbling her food.

"This isn't too bad," Jenny said, picking up Julianna's work. "I had to learn to crochet when I was taken to the mission school in Juneau. I hated it at first but now I make dainty lace doilies whenever I can buy the thread. Grandmother thinks I am foolish."

"I already like the sewing but my work will never be as good as your mother's."

"Keep it up and you will be surprised what beautiful garments you can make. Tomorrow, I will give you a drinking straw made from a wing bone of a white-headed eagle. Girls are not allowed to drink water directly from a cup and don't ask me why," Jenny laughed.

"I'm learning to just accept the rules. But a white-headed eagle bone. That is funny." Julianna and Jenny both laughed and Julianna began to appreciate the light-hearted attitude this kind woman was taking to the strict teachings of her people.

"Now you must be weary. You will sleep in that hut." Jenny pointed to a brush structure with its door open to the sea. It was very small, only enough room to sleep in.

Julianna slept peacefully that night, strangely happy in her new role as a student of the Tlingits. During her dreams she sewed dozens of moccasins, beaded in beautiful patterns.

When she woke, Jenny and the old grandmother were already sitting about a fire near her brush hut.

"You must put this on now," Jenny said, handing a strange-looking bonnet to Julianna. The big hat was beautifully decorated with ribbons and shells.

Julianna put the bonnet on. The brim of the hat was so wide that Julianna could not see very well.

"And I forgot to tell you that you may not look at the sky, and it is very important that you do not look directly at any young men. That is why the hat is made that way," Jenny said, helping her tie the colorful ribbons.

"It's beautiful. Who made it?"

"I wanted you to have a very special hat. I added many shells and copper ornaments so everyone will accept you as the chief's daughter."

"What do you mean that I will be a chief's daughter?"

"My mother says you could be adopted by us if you wish. Maybe she wants Split the Waves to take a wife and she sees that he is fond of you. Split the Waves is part Gunana. That means he is part Interior people and part Tlingit. It is important to her that his children are taught to be good Tlingits. I know that an English girl will not likely marry Split the Waves, but both mother and I know you have lost your family. She advised me to accept you if you continue with the training."

"I don't know what to say. I would like to stay with your people and I want to continue my work with Grandma, but I hope I will remember my own people and be able to decide whether I should return to them."

"I understand. We only want you to know that you are welcome among us and that we will give you a home as long as you wish. Enjoy your day and good luck with your sewing." Jenny started to leave but turned back. "Today, Split the Waves and Salkusta are leaving for a trading trip up the coast. They will meet you and I later at Klukwan."

"I would like to speak to them before they leave," Julianna said, jumping up.

The grandmother grabbed Julianna's arm, gesturing for her to sit down, while scolding the girl in Tlingit.

"What is she saying?" Julianna asked. "What did I do wrong?"

"She believes it is extremely dangerous for a young woman to be near the men before they go to sea. She would never let you go to see them off because it might place them in danger. But maybe you can look through the trees as they launch the boat."

"Please ask where I will find them in Klukwan," Julianna said, very anxious about losing touch with her companions.

"Don't worry. We will take you to them and by then you will be going as a woman, not a child. It will be a very special time for you. When I became a young woman I was soon married," Jenny smiled.

"Everyone thinks I need to be married. First, I have to remember who I am."

"We will help you find your people, my young friend. Now back to work."

"First, I want to see them leave." Julianna peeked through the trees to watch several men, including Split the Waves, push a huge boat off the shore. Salkusta's shoulder had healed, allowing the young man to join the paddlers. The craft was about fifty feet long, hollowed out from a large cedar tree and decorated with art work. It was more beautiful than any boat she had ever seen.

As they launched, the boat-men jumped into the craft two at a time and took a position on opposite sides of the boat, standing up, each with a long paddle. A man at the stern handled the sweep, a long oar that reached out behind the boat. There were about twenty paddlers, and the boat sped through the water and out of sight in minutes. Julianna turned back to her work, wishing she could be in the boat, speeding out to the open sea.

The weeks passed quickly as Julianna learned to sew every kind of clothing. She was also taught to skin and tan. Soon, her stitching was almost perfect and the grandmother often smiled at her young student. Julianna learned Tlingit words and began to understand the old woman, even catching the meaning of the stories about Crow because of the gestures her teacher made as she recounted the old tales. Julianna found that the grandmother was not at all stern; rather, she had a great sense of humour. The young girl and the old woman soon spent much of their time giggling over the smallest event.

CHAPTER 8

RIVER WOMAN'S POTLATCH

The huge boat rose and fell on the waves as the strong young men sent the craft along the coast. Towering mountains and glaciers lined the shores, glistening in the brilliant sun. The boatmen paddled for eighteen hours a day, pulling ashore for a meal of herring and a brief sleep. If the leader thought there would be rain, the crew built makeshift huts for shelter. They stopped at several Tlingit villages, trading the furs and beadwork from the interior tribes for shells, oil and ornate blankets from the coastal people. For most of the trip, the skies remained clear and the days warm. As they headed up Lynn Canal, a wind blew from the south, kicking up waves that followed their boat. The rain drenched the boaters, but their steady work kept them warm, and the strong winds helped propel them to the Chilkat town of Klukwan.

Meanwhile, Julianna remained with Jenny and the grandmother in the Tlingit village on the Alsek. The old woman continued to teach her the sewing, and then how she should dress, eat and greet others. As the days passed, the old woman grew fonder of her English student. One day she told Julianna to put aside the sewing and indicated that the young woman should follow her. She led Julianna into the village and to the longhouse.

Julianna stepped down into the building. All the men were out hunting or on the ocean voyage, and the children were playing outside. The grandmother brought Julianna to the corner of the building where a blanket hung from a stick that rested on two upright poles. The blanket was partially worked and showed brightly dyed colors woven into beautiful images of various animals, with the eagle featured in the centre of the design. Threads hung straight down from the blanket and were gathered in small bundles and protected by animal bladder bags. Julianna was told to be seated to watch the weaving. The old woman knelt in front of the work. Her old fingers flew across the loom, weaving beautifully coloured yarn into an intricate pattern.

Julianna could understand simple Tlingit sentences and was told that the blanket represented the emblems of the grandmother's clan, the Eagle, and that wearing the Chilkat blanket was a sign of the position and wealth of the family. The grandmother explained that the chiefs used the blanket for dances and potlatches.

The grandmother told her that no one among the English would be given the secret of the Chilkat blanket and that Julianna must only show the weaving to others who would use it to help their people and never let the knowledge go to those who would use it just for greed. Julianna understood the great privilege that she was being given in being taught how to weave.

She promised to keep the secret ways to herself or share them with those who would use the knowledge to make the people strong.

For the next ten days, Julianna was allowed to help the grandmother weave. Her hands had to be very clean before touching the fine goat wool, and she had to concentrate on each strand to be certain there were no mistakes.

Soon the time approached for Jenny and Julianna to walk over the mountain passes to Klukwan. The day before their departure, Jenny came to wake the young woman, bringing her a bundle of clothes.

"I am giving you the traditional dress that you are now allowed to wear as a grown woman. When you put these clothes on, everyone will know you have been raised properly and that you are no longer a child." Jenny smiled as she placed the garments in Julianna's arms.

"I feel different because for the first time in my life I don't have to be rude or to defend myself over the smallest issue," Julianna admitted.

"I was changed as well. Before my seclusion, I was so shy I would never stick up for myself. If you can believe it, I was very slight when I was your age and everyone pushed me around until I was placed in the hut. And guess how long my grandmother kept me there—two years!"

"How did you stand it! Two years in a brush hut! That is your entire teenage life!" Julianna exclaimed.

"At first I thought of running away. Then I became so addicted to sewing that today I get fidgety if I am not sewing or crocheting. After my seclusion in the village, I was taken to the mission in Juneau and taught to sew clothes, crochet and read and speak English."

"It looks like it didn't hurt you. Maybe I should stay with Grandma longer. My biggest fault was my sharp tongue. I always hurt the boys I liked the most."

"I know, Split the Waves told me you needed help. You have done very well. Now put on your clothes because we have a feast prepared," Jenny announced.

"A feast for me? But I am not Tlingit. Will the people accept me?" Julianna asked.

"Grandma is the wife and the daughter of a chief. If she presents you to the potlatch, you will be accepted and honoured by everyone. Now try on your dress."

Julianna unfolded the beautifully sewn garment.

The dress was made of tan-coloured caribou skins, sewn by Jenny who had learned the Interior Indians' design. Copper ornaments adorned the collar and a row of pink beads gave the dress a delicate touch, just right for the fair-haired girl.

"You are beautiful," Jenny said. "If Split the Waves could see you, he would be asking us for your hand. Now come. They are all waiting for you. Do you remember what Grandma told you about walking into the room at a potlatch?"

"Yes, I will keep my eyes down and walk slowly," Julianna answered. "Will Grandma be there?"

"Of course, and you will make her very proud."

Jenny led the way into the longhouse. As they approached, Julianna could hear the drums. Jenny went through the door first, then Julianna stepped down the stairs, taking her time to walk quietly and gracefully into the gathering.

The tribe sat about the large inner room. Julianna was led to a seat beside the old grandmother. Not once did she raise her eyes. Although she wanted to smile at the grandmother, she remained quiet and composed. The drumming and aroma of the food made her dizzy with happiness.

Food was distributed to the guests by Jenny and a group of younger women. Julianna was given the first hot food she had had for weeks. She was famished but remembered her lessons and ate slowly, taking small bites. When the meal came to an end she continued to sit quietly. Next was the distribution of gifts. One hundred blankets were given away to the guests. Julianna could not understand what was happening, but heard several people speak Split the Waves' name.

The gift-giving marked the end of the ceremony. Once the guests left, Jenny came over to fetch Julianna. She told Julianna that Split the Waves had supplied the gifts.

The grandmother struggled to get up and Julianna helped her. Then, the old woman spoke to Julianna in Tlingit, telling her that she was very pleased and that Julianna was a good Tlingit woman, very modest and very polite. Julianna understood most of what she said and felt more grown up than she had ever experienced before.

That night Julianna slept near Jenny in the longhouse, curtained off from the rest of the group by skins hung from the roof. She was so excited about her potlatch and the anticipation of leaving for Klukwan that it was difficult to sleep.

CHAPTER 9

JOURNEY TO KLUKWAN

Jenny roused Julianna early the next day. Julianna took tea and a piece of meat for the grandmother, realizing that this might be the last time she would see her elderly teacher. The old woman was also sad this morning, knowing that the day marked an end to her close relationship with the English-speaking girl.

Julianna sat with the grandmother and waited to fetch her more tea and to take her bowls away at the end of the meal.

"Remember to be kind to those you love as you have been kind to me and Jenny," the grandmother said to Julianna.

"Thank you." Julianna kissed her wrinkled forehead and couldn't hold back her tears. Stepping back, Julianna noticed there were also tears in the eyes of the old Tlingit elder.

Jenny and Julianna started over the trail early in the day. They carried dried salmon, flour and tea for the journey. Both wore their old clothes. Julianna was dressed in pants and a jacket and Jenny wore a cloth skirt. The beautiful ceremonial outfit was carefully packed in a waterproof container made from an animal stomach. They walked for four days over the mountains and down into the valley of the Chilkat River. It was mid-day, in the hot sun, when they spotted the river. They ran down the hill, anxious to reach the trail that would lead them to Klukwan. Instead of a shallow stream, the Chilkat River was in flood.

"Hmm," Jenny pondered the problem. "I hear you're a very good water person. Well, maybe we will have to make a raft and put you to the test."

"Let's do it!" Julianna was enthusiastic because she was aware that once they crossed the river, it would be only a few hours' walk to Klukwan and reunion with her companions.

The two women fastened straight lengths of driftwood together using pieces of rope. Soon they had a small makeshift raft, a slender pole and two rough paddles.

They stepped onto the raft. The water was high and quickly grabbed the light craft, sending the boat downriver. Julianna remained calm. She stood on the raft and angled it upstream.

"Now paddle hard!" she yelled at Jenny. They dug their paddles in, trying their best to move the raft across the river. However, the fast current swept them downstream. By the time they landed on the other side of the Chilkat River, they were near the ocean. When they stepped out on the banks, they were a short walk from the Alaskan town of Haines, thirty kilometres downstream from Klukwan.

Split the Waves had given Julianna a small purse of gold for supplies, so they went into town to buy food before starting on the trail to Klukwan. The docks were piled with gear being unloaded from boats, and the town buzzed with activity. Here, they were met by a strange sight.

"What on earth is that?" Julianna exclaimed, pointing to a herd of animals held in a fenced area. As they walked closer, they saw more of the same animals being hoisted out of the holds of a ship and lifted onto shore to be herded into the enclosure.

"They look a bit like our caribou, but they can't be. No one would ship caribou here," Jenny replied. "Let's find out. There is some kind of craziness going on."

They sought out one of Jenny's relatives.

"It's amazing," the man told her, "but these are reindeer from Lapland. They were shipped across the Atlantic, then by train across the United States to Seattle, up the coast by ship, and now they will be taken over our trail to Trondek."

"Why would anyone do that?" Jenny asked.

"Last winter the gold miners were starving in the Klondike, and the smart government people decided to send them five hundred reindeer."

"That's pretty silly. The animals won't have anything to eat on the way and besides, the steamers have already gone up the Yukon River with lots of food. This entire country appears to have lost its reason. I think I had better take my young friend and leave this madness," Jenny quipped.

It was mid-day when Julianna and Jenny started along a trail that followed the Chilkat River to Klukwan. The two companions hiked quickly, starting off at a brisk pace. Julianna was anxious to see Split the Waves, and Jenny looked forward to visiting her friends and relatives. They thought about the hot meal and companionship that awaited them. It was evening when they spotted smoke rising above the trees and they ran the last stretch into the settlement.

The village was a welcome and beautiful sight. Two rows of log houses faced the Chilkat River, and the long dug-out canoes were tied up on the riverbank. Julianna thought it was the most attractive village she had ever seen.

"They'll be in there," Jenny called out breathlessly, pointing to a large log house with carved figures guarding the entrance. They caught their breath for a moment before entering the potlatch house.

They stepped through the entrance, adjusting their eyes to the dark interior. Instead of a joyous gathering, Elders sat in a circle in somber discussion. Julianna saw Split the Waves looking drawn and worried. He came over, put his arms first around Jenny and then Julianna.

"Salkusta's loved one is going to marry another, and he left intending to kill himself. We do not know where he is and think it is likely too late to save him. One of the Elders saw him take a boat down the river. He had no paddles and appeared wild."

"Why has Katu broken their engagement?" Julianna asked. "She loved him, didn't she?"

"It was not Katu. She was sold to an old white guy for five thousand in gold. That is the story we heard from a trader who arrived this morning from the Trondek people. Salkusta is planning to let the ocean take him. It is the worst death for a Tlingit because he will be lost to the sea and his soul will never be at rest," Split the Waves said, obviously upset.

"The Elders have been discussing this and have agreed that I should take some young men and try and find Salkusta," Split the Waves continued.

"I want to come with you, please," Julianna pleaded, hating to be parted from Split the Waves once again.

"It is the same rule. No women," Split the Waves said. "But I wish you could come. I have missed you too."

"I'll paddle by myself. I saw a small dug-out on the bank. Would it be all right if I take that?"

"You will be considered pretty odd by my relatives, but then I already told them that you are called River Woman so they will understand."

Ten young men pushed the big canoe into the Chilkat and powered into the fast water. Julianna could not keep up even though she paddled with all her strength. The June waters were so swift that they were soon at the mouth of the river and paddling into the salt water.

The ocean was rough, tossed by a strong southerly wind that blew up the Lynn Canal. Clouds made it difficult to see, and Julianna had trouble following the canoe that carried Split the Waves and his companions. Then, far out in the ocean she saw something bobbing up and down in the huge waves. Julianna called out, asking Split the Waves to wait for her. She was tired and hot as she paddled over to Split the Waves' canoe.

"Look over there! Could that be him?"

Split the Waves peered through the clouds and saw a tiny speck about two kilometres out in the ocean.

The big boat sped through the water, but again Julianna's small craft slipped behind. The Tlingit canoe pulled up alongside Salkusta's small craft, and Split the Waves talked to his distraught friend. A few minutes later Julianna arrived, puffing and sweaty from the effort.

"We will get her back, Salkusta. Believe me," Split the Waves said. "Now return to the village with us, please."

"I don't have five thousand to pay for her, and if I steal Katu, she will be dishonoured. She may already be the wife of the old man. He left weeks ago. It's no use," Salkusta sobbed. "Just leave me alone."

"I have the money. I brought more than five thousand in gold nuggets from my trading trip to Trondek. Remember all those deals I made? I'll pay for her. Now what other lame arguments do you have?"

Julianna pulled up beside Salkusta and spoke quietly to him.

"Salkusta, you must follow your loved one until you have no breath left. That is what she would want."

Salkusta looked at Julianna's earnest face.

"You will come back with us now?" Julianna continued. Salkusta nodded his head.

Salkusta joined the men in the big boat. Then, the two boats began the arduous journey across the windy bay and upriver against the current. Julianna had walked for many hours that day and now faced an hour of ocean paddling and a three-hour struggle against the swift current. Her boat dropped behind, and she stopped paddling to give her arms a rest. Big waves rolled up the inlet. Although Julianna was no longer moving forward, she had to keep her paddle in the water so the small dug-out would not be swamped by waves. The big boat was far ahead, a distant speck entering the mouth of the river.

I have to make it! she told herself. Julianna had not eaten supper, and her strength was sapped. With her small reserve of energy, she dug her paddle into the waves. But her progress was slow, and the midnight sun had dipped below the horizon and returned by the time she reached the river. Julianna pulled onto shore for a brief rest. She stretched her tired arms, hoping that she would have enough strength to fight against the current. *All right, remember you are a tough woman now,* she told herself.

Julianna got back in the dug-out and began the long struggle upriver. The warm June weather had melted the snow in the mountain, raising the water level and increasing the speed of the Chilkat. She continued on for two hours until her arms ached so badly that she could not take another stroke. There was a big eddy on the riverbank where she was able to avoid the current and rest in the quiet water along the shore. This time she stayed in the boat, sheltered from the wind. *They'll be hours ahead of me if I sleep,* she thought, *but I just can't go on.* She huddled in the boat and was asleep in minutes.

"Well, River Woman, you'd better find some more muscles." It was Split the Waves smiling at her from the big boat. Julianna woke with a start.

"Will you be angry if I suggest you come with us?" Split the Waves asked. The big boat had turned back when the young men realized Julianna was no longer following behind.

"But isn't it against the rules to have a woman in the boat?" Julianna asked.

"There are exceptions. One is a beautiful maiden who needs food and rest. What do you think, River Woman?" Split the Waves put out his hand and held her small boat alongside the fifty-foot craft.

"I would be delighted to join you," Julianna said with relief, "providing I am allowed to paddle as well."

She tied the dug-out onto the big boat and joined Split the Waves and his friends. They gave Julianna a snack of dried salmon and a drink. This food was all she needed to revive her, and soon she was happily paddling along with the strong young men, entranced by the graceful rhythm of the paddlers.

The wind abated and the sky cleared. By the time they reached the village, the morning sun was sending rays of pink light over the mountain tops. Julianna was too excited to sleep and wanted to talk to Split the Waves. The central fire burned in the longhouse, and a huge iron pot of soup hung over the hot coals. They helped themselves to food and sat about the fire.

"I can't believe that Katu could be sold to an old man," Julianna said. "How could anyone do something like that?"

"Everything is changing now that the gold miners have poured in. Families in our tribe would not sell their daughters, but I heard about this happening along the route to Trondek. Gold and greed causes it," Split the Waves explained.

"Surely her family wouldn't do such a thing," Julianna continued.

"Katu is the daughter of the Han chief. But he died last year, and she was left in the care of her aunt whose husband has been caught by the evil of drink. Katu's uncle bargained a good price for Katu—five thousand in gold, twenty guns, clothing and blankets and a year's supply of food. The swindler who bought her went to Skagway to pick up these things. He's on his way over the trail now."

"Then we can catch him before he is able to take Katu away," Julianna said in a determined voice.

"I told Salkusta that we would save Katu. But I said that to save my friend from throwing himself in the ocean. The swindler left Skagway two weeks ago. If he travels as fast as the Indians, he will be in Trondek before we are at the beginning of the pass. From Dyea, we still have two days of walking and maybe ten days on the Yukon River."

"But we must try to catch him. I couldn't bear the thought of her marrying an old man that she hates and losing her true love. We must try to catch up with him."

"Salkusta is getting our gear ready right now and wants to leave within the hour. I told him that you must sleep first. So rest, my River Woman, and I will wake you when we are packed and ready to travel."

CHAPTER 10

THE KLONDIKE GOLDRUSH

It seemed as if she had just closed her eyes when Split the Waves brought her a cup of tea and a big helping of stewed salmon and bannock.

"Eat well. This may be the last hot food we enjoy for two weeks." He watched Julianna as she ate slowly, taking small bites.

"You aren't wolfing your food down like the dogs. Grandma taught you well," Split the Waves laughed. "Anyway, I liked you even when you ate all your food in two gulps."

Julianna dressed in the now-ragged clothing that she had been wearing when Split the Waves first found her, and went out into the bright sunshine to join her companions. The scene looked like an expedition to the ends of the earth. Packs of supplies were piled on the ground and ten young Tlingit men were milling about. Split the Waves and Salkusta were talking to the group. Julianna understood enough Tlingit to make out that the people were being hired to paddle them over to Dyea and then pack the trade goods over the pass.

Before they left, she hugged the woman who had been her companion for the past few weeks. "Jenny, you have been both a mother and sister to me," Julianna said just before leaving. The warm-hearted woman hugged Julianna and wished her well on their journey.

The supplies were loaded in the massive ocean-going canoe. The paddlers lined up on either side. As graceful as Greek athletes, they gave a push to the heavily loaded boat, and the first pair jumped in. Then the next pair pushed the boat forward another few feet into the river and took their places. Julianna and Split the Waves were the last set of paddlers to jump in. Salkusta sat in the stern, working the sweep. Julianna didn't ask why she was being allowed to go in the boat this time but decided that their journey to Dyea was not dangerous and that she posed little threat.

The ocean was smooth and the day pleasantly warm. With a boatful of strong paddlers, the distance from Klukwan to Dyea was quickly covered. As they approached Dyea Bay, they saw what appeared to be an armada of boats. The big ships were anchored a mile offshore, and scows and smaller boats plied the shallow waters. There were men walking up to their waists in the sea water and teams of horses pulling fully loaded wagons through the shallow, muddy waters of the tidal flats. The Tlingit boat-men slowed their pace to avoid the many boats and supplies in the bay.

"The gold miners are still arriving," Split the Waves explained.

"They are as thick as the bugs on a warm summer day," Salkusta chimed in, "and I think they will be much more trouble."

"It's the Klondike Goldrush," Julianna said.

"You mean Trondek," Salkusta corrected her.

"Yes, I guess so. I remember that twenty thousand gold miners went over the Chilkoot Pass in 1898. It's so strange because I thought I read that in a book, yet it is happening right now."

"Most of them have already gone. They landed at Dyea as soon as the news of the gold strike reached Seattle, and the rush continued all through last winter. The gold miners that made it over the pass waited on the other side of the mountains till the ice melted. These are the late comers," Split the Waves continued as they closed in on the crazed scene.

"How do you know all this?" Julianna asked. "You've been at your grandma's village and then on the Alsek River and trading along the coast."

"Hey, we know what happens in our country. Lots of my cousins were packing for the miners, earning big money. Someone in our village is always travelling from the Yukon River over to Klukwan and back. The stories travel much faster than the gold miners who are loaded down with piles of beans, some with chairs they bring all the way from Seattle, and some even bring their boats from across the ocean to pack over the pass. They are crawling, and we are running. You will see, River Woman, when we are on the trail with them."

"This time I have to speak with the white people because only they will know where the swindler is," Salkusta announced. "He's a big fat man, with greasy hair, wearing fancy watch. That is all I know, but I will get that man and say that he won't have my Katu or I kill him."

"You could be in real trouble if you killed a white man, Salkusta," Split the Waves cautioned.

"Remember, Salkusta, that you want to marry Katu. I think I will watch you closely so you don't do anything foolish and leave her weeping for you all the days of her life," Julianna said.

"I keep my knife in its scabbard. Don't worry. I just want to kill him, but I won't."

"Oh no!" Julianna yelled. "Look at that poor horse!"

There was a huge crane on the deck of the boat. It swung over the bay holding a horse in a crate. The bottom of the crate opened and the white horse dropped into the water. The poor animal sank, then surfaced, gasping and struggling. It swam back to the ship and tried to find a grip to get on board. Its hooves banged against the slippery sides of the boat. Passengers on the boat yelled at the horse and threw empty cans at its head to get the desperate animal away from the boat. Finally, the horse turned and began swimming to shore. It was a long swim to the beach. Half-way to safety, its hind end sank in the water. Soon only its head was above water. It thrashed about, not able to make any progress. By this time, the fast-moving boat with the Tlingit paddlers was close to the drowning horse.

"Save it please!" Julianna pleaded with her companions.

Salkusta moved the sweep and angled the boat just ahead of the horse. Julianna and Split the Waves went to the stern and grabbed the horse's head and placed it on the back of the boat. They held onto the collar and the horse stopped panicking and let itself be dragged to safety, feeling secure once again in the presence of humans who so recently had treated it like a piece of luggage.

The paddlers slowly brought the boat to shore. The horse was so exhausted it lay in the shallow water panting. Julianna and Split the Waves waited until the poor animal was able to stagger to its feet. In a few minutes the horse was grazing in the lush forest.

"They must be crazy to treat an animal in such a way," Julianna said indignantly.

"There will be good and bad as we mix with this crowd. I've packed for the white people before. Once I was treated so well, it was like a vacation. Another time I was treated like I was a criminal and thief, so I left the miserable man's supplies on the trail and bid him good-bye," Split the Waves recounted. "But now it is time for us to pack. Let's get on the trail and away from this dirty town."

The ten Tlingit packers sorted out the loads, giving the heaviest to the stronger men. They hoisted their loads and placed a "tump" strap across their foreheads to take a good part of the load. For some of the packers, one hundred pounds seemed to be a light chore. Earlier in the year, one of the men had packed one hundred and sixty pounds over the pass, earning forty dollars for the two days of work.

Julianna was still wearing her rafting clothes. She had a light pack that consisted of her new dress, some food, extra clothing and a sleeping robe. Hanging from her shoulder was a goat bladder filled with water. Split the Waves, Salkusta and Julianna led the way, having agreed with the packers that the group would meet at Sheep Camp that evening. With their heavy loads, they would not be able to keep the pace set by Split the Waves, Salkusta and Julianna. Speed was important. Julianna was anxious to talk to the Klondikers to try and find her family, and Salkusta wanted to find someone who knew the swindler. Split the Waves wanted information on both topics.

They moved quickly up the trail, easily overtaking the heavily burdened Klondikers. Even the horses moved slowly, trying to negotiate the downfall and the mud. The young travellers reached Finnegan's Point, where a group of Klondikers had set up their camp. The women in the group looked at Julianna with disgust and whispered among themselves.

Julianna was conscious of their disapproval.

"The worse thing a white woman can do, in their minds, is to marry an Indian," Split the Waves explained. "That is why they stare at you and make ugly faces as if you were not a fine woman. You are much finer, so don't let them bother you."

"My clothes are dreadful and so different," Julianna said, comparing her tattered pants and windbreaker to the long, stylish dresses the more well-to-do women were wearing.

"We can dress you in fancy white women's clothes, no problem. I have lots of these to trade to the women in Trondek, or Klondike as you call it. If you want to find out about your family, you should dress like them and stay away from me."

"I agree, but I don't want to stay too far away from you," Julianna said, smiling at her companion, "maybe just an hour or so when we get into Sheep Camp."

As the trail wound over rocky outcrops, the three hikers did not slow their pace. Although it was late afternoon, the sun was still high in the northern sky and beat down on them as they leapt up the steep incline.

"What is this?" Julianna had come upon an old woman lying on the trail. A boy, about ten years old, sat sobbing beside her.

"Please help me. My grandmother told me she did not feel well and sat down on the rock. Then she just fell over onto the trail. Can you do something?" the boy cried.

Her belongings were spread out over the trail and had rolled down the rocky cliff. The elderly woman looked pale but was still breathing. Julianna splashed water on her fingers and gently moistened the old woman's brow. This action brought the grandmother around. She opened her eyes and looked at them in a daze.

"Grandma! You passed out. Are you all right?" the young boy asked anxiously.

"I'm fine, John. In fact, I feel like I've had a well-needed rest."

With help from Julianna and Split the Waves, the old woman sat up.

"Here, rest on the rock for a minute and drink some water," Julianna advised.

"Maybe you need to eat a little," Salkusta said, pulling out a piece of dried salmon. "You like a piece too?" he said, smiling at John.

The boy tasted the fish. "Mmm, it's like candy. Thank you, sir." John continued to eye Salkusta, admiring the Tlingit's beaded clothing, the knife and the bow and quiver of arrows.

After the grandmother drank some water and chewed on the salmon, colour came back to her cheeks. "Thank you very much, children. I think I will be fine now. Could you help me put the pack on?"

They picked up the scattered items and fastened the load together.

When Julianna lifted the pack, she struggled to raise it onto the elderly woman's back. Split the Waves noticed and gave her a hand.

"This is much too heavy," Split the Waves said. "You should have a packer. Even River Woman who is mighty strong does not carry that much weight, and even me and Salkusta are travelling light."

"I have to pack this load and twenty more like it. Half of our supplies are still at Canyon City. I have many more trips to make."

"It's too much for Grandma," John said. He also carried a heavy pack.

"Don't worry them," the grandmother said. "They are in a rush. I can tell. We will make it eventually. Now go on your way, and God bless you for helping me."

The three hikers left reluctantly, conscious that the swindler was days ahead and that even this brief delay was putting more distance between them. They did not want to leave the old woman but were anxious to press on. They continued down the trail but after a few feet, Julianna glanced back to see how the woman was managing.

The grandmother had stopped on the trail and seemed to weave back and forth. John held her arm, worried that she would fall again. Julianna ran back, with Split the Waves and Salkusta following.

"Here, we must take this for you," Split the Waves said, removing the heavy load from the grandmother while Salkusta took John's pack.

"Thank you. Bless you all. It was too heavy for me," she said, sighing in relief.

"Do you think you can make it to Sheep Camp now or do you want to rest first?" Julianna asked.

"You go ahead, and I will come along slowly with John. My supplies are piled at this end of the camp and you will recognize them because I tied a gingham ribbon on each sack. I will meet you there. And thank you again for saving an old woman from her foolishness."

"You are not foolish at all, and when we get to camp there is something I need your advice on," Julianna said, before heading down the trail with Split the Waves and Salkusta. Despite his double load, Split the Waves did not slow his pace. They arrived in Sheep Camp in good time and deposited the two packs with the old woman's pile of supplies.

Although the main press of Klondikers had crossed the mountains during the winter and early spring, Sheep Camp still bustled with travellers. Tents were lined up along the river and up the hillsides. The pathways between the tents of this makeshift city were trampled and muddy. Entrepreneurs were busy offering a bed in a crowded tent for three dollars and a cup of coffee and a stale doughnut for a dollar and a half. Other businesses were disreputable and were operated by bunko men—the swindlers who preyed on the Klondikers along the Chilkoot Trail, out to take money from the unsuspecting and gullible.

"We don't go near these places, and they don't go near me because they think Indian people are all poor," Split the Waves said.

"But if we don't talk to people how do we find out about the swindler or try and find River Woman's people?" Salkusta questioned.

"We set up our camp, eat and then talk about our plans," Split the Waves suggested. "The packers have their own camp far from all this mess. Come, I show you."

"What about the grandmother? I want to make sure she arrived safely and I want to talk to her," Julianna reminded him.

"We will have supper and make you into a respectable white woman. Then we will come back."

Split the Waves led the way out of Sheep Camp to a place where the trees grew sparsely and rocks protruded. They followed a small trail up the side of the mountain. The packers' camp was located near a big rock that provided shelter from the frequent storms that descended into the valley. There were already several packers cooking their meals in small groups. They hailed Split the Waves, who seemed to know all the packers.

The three companions took out their cooking supplies and soon had a hot meal ready.

"This is tasty, Split the Waves," Julianna said. "I thought we were going to be eating dried salmon for ten days, not delicious soup and bannock."

"We may even get fresh meat now that we are in the mountains again. This is goat country. The Klondikers are too busy rushing to the gold mines to stop and hunt. There, if you look up on the mountain, you will see a hunter chasing down a goat."

"I can see someone running up the ridge of the mountain," Julianna said, straining to follow the small speck high above them. "Now I see the goat."

She watched the nimble Tlingit run across the mountain side. Then a shot rang out.

"Now you see how we are always able to cook meat over the fire," Split the Waves said.

They finished their meal and rested, waiting for the packers to arrive with the rest of the supplies. It was peaceful in this area of Sheep Camp. Julianna relished the calm and quiet, realizing that the other travellers were crammed into the small, filthy area along the Dyea River. Before long, their packers arrived, thankful that soup and bannock had been prepared for them.

"Here is your new outfit, River Woman," Split the Waves said, handing her a colourful cotton dress and bonnet. "Let me know if this fits. I have several others if you don't like this one."

"It is very nice." Julianna had ducked into the tent to change and emerged looking like a very properly dressed young woman in the late nineteenth century.

"Now you better watch those gold miners. You look so pretty they'll be asking for your hand in marriage," Split the Waves said, admiring her.

"I'll be true to you," Julianna answered with a grin. "I'm going to see the grandmother first and take her the soup and bannock. She'll be too tired to cook. I also want to get her help once she has had time to rest. People will confide in someone like her. She may know about the swindler or a fourteen-year-old girl who is missing."

Julianna walked jauntily through Sheep Camp, receiving many admiring glances from the gold miners and several unwelcome propositions. When she passed the tent with the bunko men, someone called out to her. Now she was face to face with one of the many swindlers who preyed upon the innocent.

"Hey, come work for me, gal. I'll pay you forty dollars a day."

Julianna turned towards the oily voice. It was a man in his forties wearing a slick-looking gray suit with a heavy gold chain dangling on his thin frame.

"I treat the young women properly, being that I was born in the south where a gentleman learns how to behave. The name's Jerome de Compte. From the best of families as y'all know, I am sure." His voice was like syrup and a forced smile crossed his face. But evil seeped out from behind the smile and the false gentility.

Julianna wanted to run but she had the feeling that this man might hold the secret of Katu's sale.

"I was looking for an older man, one who wears a fancy watch and is bringing lots of presents to the Klondike for his young bride," Julianna said. "Do you know that man by any chance?"

"Maybe I do. Maybe I don't. What is it worth to you? If you come work for me, I might just remember this guy's name. What you think about that, my pretty one?"

Julianna wanted to run from this devious, conniving snake. Instead, she played along. "I will think it over. But first I must bring this food to a friend. I will come back if I think it will be worthwhile."

Julianna couldn't wait to get out of his sight. She felt soiled just speaking to the man. She rushed through the camp to locate the grandmother.

The old woman was resting while John searched through their food bag for supplies for supper.

"There is my guardian angel!" the grandmother said as Julianna approached on the trail.

"I've brought you some food, but I've also come to seek your help. Here, share the soup and bannock with John before it gets cold. While you eat, I will tell you my problem."

"This is very good of you," she said. "John, there are bowls and spoons in the brown pack. Now what is the problem, dear? I will do whatever I can to help."

"I've lost my family. Actually, I've lost my memory and do not know who I am except that I think I used to live in Whitehorse because that name seems so familiar to me. Do you know of anyone who lost a daughter?"

"No dear, I have not heard of any family missing a daughter, but I can ask the other travellers."

"We have another problem. Salkusta is mad with grief because his betrothed has been sold to the swindler. Among the Tlingit we only know him as 'the swindler.' We have a description of what he looks like. I really don't think I will find my family until my memory comes back, but I do want to help Salkusta catch up to the swindler. The dreadful man in the bunko tent seems to know who he is. He wants me to work for him in exchange for information."

"Be very careful of those men. They are all in league with Soapy Smith and very dangerous. You must have heard about Soapy. He runs Skagway and steals from every unsuspecting Klondiker. He and his gang of thieves promise money and fancy clothes in order to entrap young girls. The ones unfortunate enough to believe their lies become lost women."

"Don't worry about me. I wouldn't get taken in by that slime. But I need your help. If you come with me, we could work together to get some information from him. Oh, I forgot to tell you, I am called River Woman."

"I am Mrs. Hannah, and this is my grandson, John," she replied. "Now the first thing we should do is give you another name for the time being. How would Marie do?"

"Good. I like that. It makes me feel comforted. Maybe I knew someone called Marie." She paused for a minute to try and capture a fleeting memory from the past, then continued her conversation with Mrs. Hannah. "While we walk over, could you tell me why you are taking this difficult trip?"

"It's a long story," Mrs. Hannah continued, "and not a happy one. John's father left for the Klondike two years ago, leaving my daughter, Sarah, and their son, John, with me. I was well off with my own home and had no problem caring for them, although my dear Sarah was often ill. Letters arrived from the Klondike, and then last year we received a note from the bank informing us that my son-in law had deposited fifty thousand dollars in trust for his wife and son. His older brother was named as the executor of the funds. Two weeks after the good news about the huge fortune, we received word of my son-in-law's death. My daughter Sarah took to her bed and died within three weeks of hearing the dreadful news."

Mrs. Hannah continued, "I could have coped with all of this, although I was terribly distraught over the deaths of my lovely daughter and dear son-in-law. But another blow struck us. His brother became greedy once he had the money under his control. He went to the courts and had me declared incompetent. My house was taken from me, and they were about to take John. I was to be placed in a home for the destitute and John in a home without love. We had only one hope. With the news of my son-in-law's death, we received notice of the mining claim. It will expire in September of this year, and John and I intend to pay the back royalties and reclaim it."

"What an amazing story. You are a very brave person, Mrs. Hannah. It's so strange. We are rushing to the Klondike to save Katu from marrying the swindler and you are rushing to the Klondike to save young John's fortune from swindlers. I hope the entire Klondike Goldrush is not just an army of criminals and thieves."

"There are many good people on the trail. The evil ones are the exception. Most people share their food and help one another out, just the way you and your friends helped me out."

As they walked to the bunko tent, Mrs. Hannah and Julianna discussed their plan. There were several unsuspecting customers in the tent when Julianna and Mrs. Hannah approached. The two woman waited just outside the tent, listening to Jerome's pitch.

"Now you good men just rest yourselves and take a cup of hot coffee. We are all going to be rich in the Klondike, but we should have a little fun on the way there. My family has more money than I need. A southerner, y'all must know. So I'm here to cheer y'all up and share a little of my money. It's as easy to win from me as taking candy from a babe. Do you fancy a little game while you rest?" His voice was oil mixed with syrup, and he spoke with an affected southern drawl.

The three gold miners nodded their heads and stepped up to the gaming table.

"You're bright gentlemen, you are," the bunko man continued. "Now just watch the pea and put out your wager. If you guess which shell hides the pea, I pay you twice your money."

The miners guessed but the pea wasn't there.

"Oh, too bad, my good men," the oily voice exclaimed. "The next time you'll be winners."

But in that game, the pea was always pushed between a crack in the table and then recovered under the shell they had not picked. After fifteen minutes the three men came out, with dismayed expressions, either grumbling that the game was fixed or blaming themselves for risking their dwindling funds.

The bunko man noticed the two women at the tent door.

"Ah my ladies, come in and I'll get y'all some coffee. Glad to see the young lady brought her mother to bargain a good price for such a beauty."

"We are here to bargain but not for Marie," Mrs. Hannah stated firmly. "We saw your little trick with the pea and intend to inform everyone in Sheep Camp and the authorities at the border unless, of course, you provide us with the information we seek."

For a minute the smooth-talking villain could not think of a reply. Then his devious mind clicked back into action.

"If you do that, I will inform everyone that Miss Marie is a prostitute and that you were trying to sell her to me for too high a price. Everyone saw the young woman belongs to an Indian, and they would have no trouble believing my story over yours."

But just at that time Split the Waves joined them and heard this insult. He was infuriated.

"You are scum who bring filth to my country. This young woman has been adopted by my people when she lost her family. She is a high-ranking Tlingit now and if you should ever speak that way again, my people will deal with you when you return to your hellhole in Skagway. We have nothing to fear from you and do not wish to bargain for information from a thief. We are going to spread the news of your treachery."

Split the Waves started off but was hailed back by Mrs. Hannah. "Wait, I think he is ready to tell us what he knows. Is that not right?"

"What is it then? You want the name and location of Mr. Crump? Well, you'll never catch him. He left Sheep Camp two weeks ago and at Lake Lindeman he hired Gaston and the Kid—two of the strongest river men in all of Alaska and the Yukon. They go in a boat called the *Devil's Own*. They will be half-way to the Klondike by the time you reach the summit. Now get away from my tent!"

"Let's tell Salkusta. He has been asking everyone about the swindler and learned nothing. Now we have a name and the boat to look for," Julianna exclaimed.

They located Salkusta and John and walked Mrs. Hannah back to her tent. Julianna gave her Tlingit friends a brief account of the treachery that had befallen Mrs. Hannah and John. The young men were incensed at the unfairness the old woman had been subjected to.

"You will never make it to the Klondike before the water freezes if you are going to pack the rest of your supplies up from Canyon City," Split the Waves calculated. "Then it will be dangerous for you on the river because freeze-up can start, and you may be caught in the ice if you are still travelling in October. There is just not enough time for you to make a safe trip."

"I don't have a choice," Mrs. Hannah explained. "I sold my jewellry to buy our passage. My house was worth ten thousand and I had bonds worth five thousand, and it was all taken from me. I am poor in funds but rich in having my grandson. We will manage somehow, even if we don't save the claim. I can cook and do laundry."

They helped pitch Mrs. Hannah's tent and left her to rest.

"I need to talk to you in private," Split the Waves said, beckoning to Salkusta. "I want to give some of the gold to the old woman, but then we will not have all the five thousand to pay for Katu. What do you think?"

"But I can't lose her. It would be worse than death to have her marry that ugly old man!"

"I give you my word that we will rescue her even if we steal her away or throw the swindler into the Kwanlin Dun where the waves are the biggest. The old woman has been sent to us for a purpose," Split the Waves added.

"I feel that too. John looks to me like I'm his older brother or maybe the father he lost. Yes, I agree and I trust you and I trust myself to save Katu, somehow." Salkusta's face was strained but he sounded strong and determined.

"Okay, we give gold to the boy because the old woman will not take it," Split the Waves said, motioning John and Julianna to join them.

"You must help your grandmother get the supplies over the pass as soon as possible, or your lives will be in danger trying to get down the river when the ice comes. Here is enough gold to send her supplies on the tram from Canyon City and to lift the bags in Sheep Camp up to the Summit. You must help though."

"What can I do?"

"You know that half your supplies are still in Canyon City? Take this much of the gold," Split the Waves said as he dug several nuggets from the poke, a small leather bag holding the gold. "Give this to the tramway operators and show them where your gear is piled. They are honest businessmen and won't cheat you. Don't show your gold around because not everyone is honest. You have a long run down to Canyon City and back. When you return, put your supplies on the tram up at the scales. It will go to the top in minutes, and by tomorrow night you and your grandmother and all your belongings will be on the summit. I will send my packers back to take you and your grandmother to Bennett Lake, and they will help you build a boat to take you downriver."

"Why are you doing this?" the young boy asked.

"We don't know why," Salkusta replied. "We just feel it is something we have to do. Now start on your way to Canyon City. Take a bit of food and make fast time before I tell Split the Waves to take back the gold." Salkusta gave the young boy a playful punch. "You be in the Klondike soon, John. Come and see me."

The three companions had mixed feelings as they returned to their tents. Salkusta worried that the thousand in gold could not be replaced. Split the Waves puzzled over the various prospects for replenishing his gold supply, and Julianna wondered if there was any way she could bring in money. One thousand! It seemed like a fortune.

Although they were concerned about the diminished supply of money, it gave them a warm feeling thinking of Mrs. Hannah and John walking up the steep pass unencumbered by heavy packs.

They slept briefly and began the ascent just as the sun rose to herald another long June day. The path led out of the tangled vegetation and onto the approach to the pass. They snaked upwards, passing huge boulders, which looked like a field of stone houses. There were a few pine trees and then only rock, melting ice and trickling water. The scene was breathtaking. Bright mountain flowers covered every crack. Above, the mountain tops reflected the pink sunrise.

Ahead of them were the steps cut into the ice. This ascent over the pass was called the Golden Stairs. Despite it being very early in the morning, there was already a steady stream of gold miners inching their way up the steep incline. Although the main press of Klondikers had passed through earlier that spring, there were still a thousand travellers on their way to the summit. The three companions fell in behind and began the long, steady climb. They carried small packs and were able to enjoy the ascent. Ahead, their fellow travellers on the trail grunted and wheezed from the stress of carrying fifty to one hundred pounds up an ascent that was so steep in places that the hikers had to cling to the rocks with both hands.

By the time they reached the summit, the sun was high overhead in a bright blue sky. They were happy to break away from the slow train of Klondikers and begin the quick descent. The Klondikers were delayed by the Mounted Police who checked their supplies and levied a custom tax.

"Don't we have to pay?" Julianna asked.

"This is my country," Split the Waves replied. "They don't bother us. Two years ago the Chief of the Tlingits allowed the Klondikers to pass through when big officials came to talk to him. Before that no white man was allowed on the Chilkoot Trail. Maybe a few sneaked by, but not many because it is our trail. If a policeman tried to get money from the Tlingits who have used this trail from before my grandmother or my grandmother's mother, there would be pretty big trouble."

"Why did you want to keep the white people out in the first place?" Julianna asked.

"Hey, she don't understand at all what is going on," Salkusta laughed, "and I was just beginning to believe she was good Tlingit woman."

Julianna knew it was just friendly chiding and did not take offence. "All right, you two, tell me so I won't ask dumb questions."

"Don't pay attention to Salkusta," Split the Waves said. "You know plenty about our people. You just need to know a bit more. We Tlingits are traders and make lots of money bringing furs, skins and moccasins to the white traders. Then at ports like Skagway, we buy white people's goods to bring back across the mountains, to the Indian people you call 'Sticks.'"

"Sticks. I've never heard that before," Julianna replied.

"They call themselves Tagish Kwan, the Han, the Touchone, the Kaska—all the people that live along the Yukon River and further inland," Split the Waves explained.

"I heard of those native groups," Julianna said.

"Anyway, a long time ago the Hudson's Bay Company came into our trading area, not from the coast, but from inland rivers, and built Fort Selkirk. My grandfather told me how angry his people were about this. They sent our traders to tell the white people to get out but they didn't go until we burned down the fort."

"You what?" Julianna was shocked.

"So you are just going to react like the white people now." Salkusta was still laughing at Julianna. He never intended to hurt her but loved to tease.

Julianna had left behind the sharp tongue that always got her in trouble, but this time she was tempted to tell them what savages they were.

"We aren't savages," Split the Waves said, as if he could read Julianna's thoughts. "My people were protecting their livelihood. I will try to explain. Let's imagine that your father had a good business on his own property. Then your family goes away on a buying trip and when you return, someone else has put up a competing store right on your father's land. Your father tells this guy to get off his land but the thief won't move. Your father would get a lawyer and get the police and if he still didn't go, they would burn the building down. Do you understand now what the Chilkats did?"

"The Tlingits depended on trade in order to buy flour and sugar and western clothing and once the white people took that over, they would become poor. But how do you know so much about my people," Julianna asked, "like how they do business and own land and get lawyers and have police officers?"

"See, we are not dumb. When I pack for the gold miners, I always ask questions. At first, I can barely speak well enough, but now I understand more and can explain in your English."

"I agree you are both pretty smart. So if you are so clever, how are we going to build a boat and still catch up with Crump and his gang?" Julianna asked with a chuckle.

"You are going to feel bad again, River Woman, because we won't be building a boat or raft and wasting our time at Lindeman. Salkusta, you and I will take a boat that we left hidden in the trees. So no problem. We will be at Lindeman very soon and get in the water. There is good white water that you will have fun to paddle."

CHAPTER 11

THE KLONDIKE ARMADA

They dropped into the valley and soon reached Lake Lindeman. Tents were erected throughout the bottom land and Klondikers were busy cutting trees. As the young travellers walked through the tent city, they could hear the men yelling at each other. One gold miner stood high on a platform, holding the top of a long saw. The other stood at the bottom, pushing the saw back up. Sawdust fell into the eyes of the man below, and the one on top often thought his partner was not doing his share to push the saw back up through the green wood. Julianna was glad they did not have to sweat over their boat building.

On the shore, a flotilla of boats took off across the lake, and on the trail there was a line of gold miners lugging their gear over to Bennett Lake.

"Maybe find us some food," Split the Waves suggested, "and Salkusta and I will get the boat. We will have a sleep here so it will give our packers a chance to catch up to us. After this, we won't rest until we reach the Tagish village."

In a few minutes they were back, dragging a good-sized dug-out. Julianna handed them a lunch of old bannock, dried fruit and meat. They found a shady spot to sleep until awakened by the packers. The Tlingit packers helped load the trading goods and pushed the dug-out into the lake, then waved from shore before retracing their steps over the pass to Sheep Camp. The three travellers were relieved to be on the water. Soon, Julianna and her two companions reached the outlet to Lake Lindeman.

"It's white water," Julianna yelled enthusiastically.

The current grabbed the boat and flung it down the rapids. Julianna was in the bow pointing the boat straight through the biggest water, and Split the Waves and Salkusta were in the stern, steering and bracing to keep from flipping. They were through in minutes, cutting off several hours of hiking over the trail. Two wrecked boats were washed up in the eddy at the end of the run, and supplies circulated in the slow water at the river's edge.

"I guess this was the end of the trip for several Klondikers," Julianna observed.

"There are some good boat-men among the miners but lots of them have never been in swift water before. Suddenly they expect to run the big waves. Too bad for them." Salkusta did not seem too sorry. To his thinking, one or two wrecked boats lessened the overwhelming influx of strangers.

They entered the quiet bay at the head of Bennett Lake and paddled along hills cleared of almost every tree. Tents were scattered everywhere, and they could hear the hammering and sawing of the boat builders.

"I don't wish to visit another mad town. Let's start for the Tagish village," Split the Waves suggested.

Julianna looked up the lake where the water disappeared into the distance. "How far do we have to go?"

"Just a few hours and we go visit good people and have some hot food. I have cousins across the lake at Caribou Crossing and more friends when we get to Tagish."

As they headed across Bennett Lake, the wind came up from the west. Huge waves crashed into the stern of the boat, washing over Split the Waves and Salkusta.

"Keep the boat straight with the wind," Split the Waves said to Julianna and Salkusta, "and I will put up a sail. Then we will be as fast as the big steam boats."

Split the Waves pulled a skin from his pack and attached it to a pole that he erected as a makeshift mast. As soon as the wind hit the sail, the boat jerked forward. They were going so fast Julianna was afraid the boat would veer sideways and flip them. They covered the forty-eight kilometres in a couple of hours. A sandy beach awaited them at Caribou Crossing. Julianna jumped out, and Split the Waves and Salkusta helped her drag the boat up on shore. They made their way over to the small cabins and tents of the Tagish people.

Split the Waves' cousins fed them caribou steaks, potatoes and dessert. After the filling meal, the three tired companions slept for an hour, first asking their hosts to wake them. Split the Waves shook Julianna from her sleep. She mumbled, "Graham! Charles! Help!" in a fretful nightmare and dropped back to sleep again.

"River Woman, we have to go now. You're having a bad dream," Split the Waves said, gently shaking her.

"Oh, I'm sorry, Split the Waves. I am so tired I can barely open my eyes," Julianna said, trying to remember what had disturbed her sleep.

"You called out for Graham and Charles," Split the Waves informed her. "Is one of these guys your betrothed?" Split the Waves tried to be light-hearted, but Julianna could detect a note of concern.

"You remind me of Graham. I can't remember him too well, but he looks a lot like you, just a little younger and maybe not as experienced with the world as you are. We were going through big water together, and I was terrified."

"It will all come back to you," Split the Waves said. "When you find out who you are, I hope you don't discover that you are already married. Please try not to worry yourself about that now. We must think about the journey ahead and try and get through Windy Arm tonight before the waves are as high as mountains."

They pushed off from Caribou Crossing and enjoyed the current that took them into Tagish Lake. Hills rose up along the lake. Ahead, the sheltered bay opened up to a large body of water. Here were the dangerous waters of Windy Arm, feared by the Klondikers. Although they were still some distance away, they could see the white caps on the water.

"We'll be okay in the waves. It is not so bad," Split the Waves assured Julianna.

"It looks bad to me. I can go through the biggest rapids on a river, but I don't feel safe in big lake water with high winds and big waves," Julianna admitted.

"Place the bow so it cuts across the wave a little off centre. That way the boat rides up and doesn't plunge deep into the trough. When you are at the top of the wave, give it a small tap to keep the bow from knifing the wave and swamping us. Salkusta and I will make sure we don't tip and help you lots. Don't worry. We will be through this bad water before morning."

Before morning, Julianna thought. *That's hours of difficult paddling!* Then Julianna experienced a flash from her past, remembering a thousand-kilometre canoe race on the Yukon River. "I guess it's possible to paddle day and night," she mumbled, recalling that fast racers completed the distance in five days, sleeping only a few hours at a time.

The trip was tough and waves pushed at them from all sides. Once they crossed behind the big island, Julianna thought they would be protected. Instead, they were in a section called Sucker Bay where they were hit by the worst of the turbulence. Winds blew at them from the south, east and west and cross waves rose unexpectedly. She struggled to keep the boat's angle. The sheltered waters always seemed to be farther in the distance. They travelled slowly and carefully. Their muscles ached, but no one complained.

For one second, Split the Waves stopped paddling to secure one of the bags. As he reached forward, the boat tipped dangerously. Salkusta braced at the stern, and Julianna dug a high brace in the bow. The boat veered to one side, and water rushed over the gunnels.

"We're tipping!" Julianna yelled, and the memory of Turnback Canyon swept over her in terrifying reality.

"No!" Split the Waves yelled, grabbing his paddle and bringing the boat to trim. "We're fine."

Julianna breathed more easily. She knew how close they had come.

"How are you doing, River Woman?" Split the Waves yelled once they had braved the waves and pushed onto the more sheltered arm of the lake.

"I'm fine. Just anxious for a good hot meal," Julianna replied.

It would be a long time before they would enjoy a break for just then, a frightened scream echoed across the water.

"A boat's capsized!" Julianna yelled.

"Turn back!" Split the Waves yelled in response.

They brought their boat around and paddled hard over to the frightened men. Two men were struggling in the water. Waves rocked the boat, making the rescue dangerous for everyone.

"Grab a line!" Salkusta called, throwing out a rope. One of the men caught the rope and pulled himself alongside the boat. Salkusta grabbed his arms and carefully pulled the big man into the boat. Salkusta threw the line out to the other man.

"Take it!" they all yelled. The man reached for the line but was so exhausted he couldn't grasp the rope. They moved closer to the drowning man and once more threw out a rope.

This time the desperate man caught the rope, and with his remaining strength held on as they pulled him to shore.

When they beached the canoe, the man lay in the water, unable to get to his feet.

Saluska dragged the victim to shore while Julianna and Split the Waves rushed to build a fire and find dry clothing for the Klondikers. One of the men was hypothermic. They covered him with warm robes and gave him a hot drink. The other man recovered quickly, and sat about the fire with his rescuers.

"Maybe you can help us," Split the Waves said. "We are looking for a boat called the *Devil's Own*. Have you seen it?"

"We are the slowest of the slow and have been passed by everyone. I couldn't miss that boat, because it was the fastest craft we saw among all the boats heading for the Klondike. There were three men on the *Devil's Own*, one older fat man who sat like a log, a big strong oarsman and a young hefty man."

"When you see them?" Salkusta asked.

"Now, let's see. As I said, we're slow even in good weather, but the waves came up on Bennett Lake and we had to hole up on shore. While we camped, the *Devil's Own* went speeding by. That would be four days ago," the Klondiker said.

"Four days!" Salkusta repeated. "We'll never catch them if we don't get back on the water!"

"Don't let us hold you up any longer," the Klondiker said. "Soon as my buddy is on his feet, we'll walk back to Caribou Crossing. Better to go back to San Francisco than risk our lives in this country."

Julianna and her three companions had not slept for more than a few hours at a time over the past three days. Somehow they were able to nap and rise feeling refreshed. The three of them said good-bye to the Klondikers and then pushed their dug-out into the water.

Julianna couldn't believe that she was going with so little sleep. Somewhere in her past she remembered sleeping late into the day, and she could imagine her mother's voice calling to wake her. Faint memories flitted through her mind and quickly faded as she paddled hour after hour—memories that showed a flash of her past but not enough for her to know who she was or where she came from.

Finally, they reached the current of Six Mile River that would take them to the Tagish village. Around every corner they hoped to catch a whiff of smoke or see tents on the shore. Their destination was the great longhouse on the banks of the river. Here, there would be food for the travellers and a place to sleep. The Tagish people were waiting for Split the Waves, anxious to get news from the Tlingit people and new supplies of clothing and goods.

"There it is!" Salkusta announced. "I am so hungry I will have to eat in gulps the way River Woman used to eat."

"I am going to wolf my food down like it was the last meal I will ever have," Julianna replied, feeling pleased that her friends liked her for who she was, not for her newly acquired manners.

They landed on the muddy banks of the river, tied up their boat and climbed up the steep slope. It was late afternoon on a warm, sunny June day. The Tagish people came down to the shore to greet them. Everyone knew Split the Waves and welcomed him. Some knew Salkusta and were pleased to see him on this trading trip. They looked Julianna over and were not sure of what to make of her. She still wore her ragged rafting clothes and her purple lifejacket. She was not a pleasant sight to the Tagish.

Split the Waves explained who Julianna was and asked that the Tagish people welcome the adopted daughter of the Tlingits. Everyone was polite, yet there was a certain reserve. Julianna understood that she was dressed too casually. She slipped away into the bushes, washed in the river, and changed into her beautiful handmade garment. When Julianna reappeared, dressed in her regalia, the Tagish people let out an appreciative sigh.

Julianna did not understand the Tagish language but sensed their feelings. They liked her dress and immediately recognized her stature with the Tlingit people by the ornate clothing.

"They love you already, River Woman. That was a smart thing to do. I should have changed my clothing, too, but I was so anxious to get some food. When we come to a village, we stop to put on our best clothes to honour the people we are visiting. It is our custom. Now Salkusta and I go to dress in our special clothes because the Tagish wish to sing and dance with us."

Julianna's excitement grew when she heard the drums booming out from the longhouse. She remembered the potlatch held for her on the Alsek River and how she had been nervous, worried she might make a mistake. Now this celebration would be different. This day, she felt strong and self-assured, ready to be part of the festivities and enjoy herself.

"You look so handsome, I think I want to marry both of you," Julianna laughed when Split the Waves and Salkusta returned beautifully dressed in decorated skin clothing. "I think you even took a bath and left behind your camp odours."

"So you have been sniffing us, have you," Split the Waves continued. "That is a good sign."

"I've flirted with you two long enough," Julianna laughed. "We should go and see if there are any rich Tagish boys who want to marry a high-ranking Tlingit woman with blond hair."

"I will be watching you," Split the Waves said as they stepped into the longhouse to join the celebration.

Split the Waves passed out gifts from his trading supplies and sat with the chief to relate the latest happenings on the trail. Julianna joined Salkusta so he could translate for her when necessary.

As the tempo of the dancing increased, Julianna did not care if she understood the conversation. She watched as the village people moved across the floor to the rhythm of the drums and the melodious high voices of the singers.

One of the women held out her hand, indicating to Julianna that she should join the dance. As Julianna moved gracefully around the room, she saw Split the Waves watching her. She smiled at him, aware that she looked attractive in the faint light and shadows of the longhouse, dressed in the beautiful soft garment.

But when Julianna glanced at Salkusta, she noticed he looked tense.

106

She realized that the chase to the Klondike was foremost on his mind. It was clear that the young man was impatient to be back on the water. When the dance ended, she joined Salkusta and asked if he wanted to leave.

"If we go before the day is over, we will make Whitehorse tomorrow morning and then can have a good sleep in Split the Waves' old cabin. It is not too far, I think," Salkusta said, anxious to be underway.

"You are kidding me again, Salkusta. I know how far it is to Whitehorse. It's days away. No one paddles from Tagish to Whitehorse overnight unless they are insane."

"Well, how far is it, River Woman, and how do you know these lakes?" Salkusta questioned in his good-humoured way. "I think Whitehorse may be part of your life. Am I right?"

"Maybe. The name sounds very familiar, but Split the Waves said it was just a small place with a few traders. My memory of Whitehorse is entirely different. I can't even tell you because you would think I have lost my mind."

"But you have lost your mind, and Split the Waves and I still like you. We are not going to throw you in big canyon at Kwanlin just because you forget who you are."

"Does the canyon have high, reddish-coloured cliffs that go straight down to the water and a small bridge across the canyon?"

"That is what the canyon walls are like, but there is no bridge. You must be making some things up when you have those dreams and talk so much in your sleep that Split the Waves has to tell you to be quiet."

"He does not. He would never say that to me," Julianna protested.

"You are right," Salkusta admitted. "He only gives you a gentle shake so the bad dreams don't disturb your sleep. He like you I think."

"And I like him too," Julianna confessed. "He reminds me of someone I knew before I lost my memory."

"I guess you had a boyfriend who is waiting for you to come back," Split the Waves said. He had been listening to the last part of the conversation and heard Julianna admit her feelings for him. He was glad that she had become so much more open with her emotions— not at all like the girl he had found on the Alsek River. He smiled at her as they loaded their canoe to head out into Marsh Lake.

It was one of those unforgettable days when the sun lingers on the mountain tops, sending glorious colours across the sky. Beauty surrounded them. The water was clear and calm, reflecting the mountains and hills along the shore. They spoke little and the only sound was the steady dipping of the paddles. They never stopped during the entire length of Marsh Lake. The paddlers got into a rhythm and kept up the pace for the four hours it took them to reach the outlet. Weary from paddling on flat water throughout the night, they were relieved to finally reach moving water. This was the beginning of the Yukon River, first slow as it moved through the marshy area leading out of the lake, and then faster as the river narrowed. The canoe sped forward towards the canyon—the biggest challenge on the voyage from Bennett City to the Klondike.

Split the Waves spotted the beginning of the canyon.

"Do we need to pull over and have a look, or is everyone ready to run the canyon?" Split the Waves asked.

"I'm fine," Julianna replied, remembering a fairly docile canyon that canoeists often paddled on a Sunday afternoon. "This is no big deal."

"My River Woman has been through here, I think," Split the Waves surmised. "I am impressed if you think this is easy water."

"I know it is bad water," Salkusta added. "I've never been through here before. My family took the portage just to be safe. This time I am in a big hurry, and I know my two super paddlers will keep me from swimming. Let's get it over with."

They sped into the canyon entrance. Julianna was not at all nervous, believing that she had been through this section before, and that it was so easy she could paddle it with her eyes closed. She was surprised when the boat was suddenly grabbed by the swift current and white water kicked up between the high walls.

"It's changed," she yelled. "We're in for it!" Julianna realized that the canyon would be almost as difficult as Turnback. Ahead was a high wave that kicked up a plume of foam. They maintained the speed of the boat as they plunged through the surging wave. Above was a bridge that spanned the most dangerous part of the canyon. Several Klondikers watched from above, cheering them on. Their boat leapt through the canyon walls and into the swirling waters below. Again, they had to use all their strength to maintain the forward motion of their boat so it would not get sucked into the whirlpool. They strained on the paddles and the boat headed into the second portion of the canyon. This part was narrow but easier to negotiate. In minutes, they were resting in an eddy, catching their breath.

"What did you think of that, River Woman?" Split the Waves asked.

"It was frightening," Julianna replied. "But how come I thought the waters were tame?"

"Maybe you come from a different time when the waters were calmer, like on the Alsek before the ice dam burst," Split the Waves kidded. "But you were correct about the bridge. It was not there last time I paddled the canyon. Now the white people have a way to cross the canyon. If you knew the bridge was built, you must have been here before."

"Maybe I come from Whitehorse," Julianna said, and then to herself she thought, *I remember a big dam downriver from the canyon, calm water in the canyon, and a reservoir behind the dam.* However, she did not share these thoughts with her companions.

"I guess Whitehorse Rapids is also big water," she said, expecting the worse.

"You're correct, and it is coming up soon. We could line the boat and pack over the supplies. Already some miners drowned here, and one man lost his gear and shot himself right there on that bank. But it is only a short trip, taking only a minute to fly through and I know how you love the big water," Split the Waves said with a smile.

"I won't shoot myself if we tip," Julianna said, "but maybe I should hike around just to keep our supplies dry."

"No, River Woman," Salkusta interrupted. "You always like to take the dangerous water. I will take a pack around and watch you and Split the Waves shoot the rapids. This is where you earned your name, right, Split the Waves?"

"I hope I do it justice, for I would not want my friend to swim."

"I hope to keep the boat pointed into the big waves and not spill you into the drink," Julianna answered.

Salkusta pushed them into the current. Immediately, they flew into the waves and had to paddle with all their strength to keep up their momentum. The boat dropped over a ledge, hit the circulating water and stalled for a second until Julianna and Split the Waves sent the boat downstream into the current. Julianna was in the bow. She gasped as the boat approached a giant wave that rose high above their heads. They drove the boat up the wave until the stern was buried and the boat was almost perpendicular. Then the bow fell into the trough. Julianna braced hard to prevent the boat from sinking out of sight. They rose out of the foam to whoops and hollers from the onlookers. Ahead, the water calmed, and they paddled over to meet Salkusta.

"Time for food and a sleep," Split the Waves announced. "My cabin is just downriver."

What used to be a quiet native fishing spot had changed over the last year. The banks of the river were lined with tents and log houses, and boats were tied so close together there was no place for them to land.

Julianna was puzzled. The river was familiar, but everything else was strange. She vaguely remembered streets and tall buildings.

"This used to be my grandfather's fishing spot," Split the Waves said, perturbed at the intrusion of outsiders.

They found a spot to pull onto the bank, tied up the canoe, and walked over to a log cabin. Smoke rose from the chimney.

Split the Waves opened the door to find three gold miners in his house.

"Hey, what are you guys doing in here?" Split the Waves demanded. "This is my grandfather's house."

"Not anymore," one of the men snarled. "Now get off with you Indians."

Julianna thought Split the Waves would fight for his home. Instead, he just shook his head and walked away.

"Why didn't you throw them out like you did at Fort Selkirk?"

"It's no use," Split the Waves answered sadly. "There are too many of them and too few of us. If I hit a white man, they will put me in jail and then we will never save Katu. I have to let it go, but it is hard to take. So what do you think of this town? Is this where your family lives?"

"No. It's not the same place. I am very disappointed because the name sounded so familiar. The river and the hills look the same, but everything else is different. I don't live here," Julianna explained in a discouraged voice.

It was a somber group that paddled downriver to find a campsite. To make matters worse, a wind came up and driving rain pelted down. It was the most dismal evening they had spent so far. Finally, they found a sandbar downriver from Whitehorse. They built a shelter with poles and fir branches and crawled under the makeshift roof for a short sleep. They had no hot food to eat and they were exhausted from the long hours of paddling. Julianna felt too sick to even nibble on dried salmon.

"We've overslept," Salkusta called out, rousing them from their sleep. "We wasted hours. We'll never catch Crump if we keep sleeping!"

"Don't worry so much," Split the Waves assured him. "How long does the Klondiker take to go over the pass and downriver? Some started last winter, and they are still on the water. We left Bennett two days ago, so we have already gained on them. Most of those white guys we saw at Lindeman won't get to Dawson until the fall."

"Remember, he has two of the strongest boatmen in the Yukon. They could be in Dawson before we get to Fort Selkirk," Salkusta said, as he hastily threw their belongings into the dug-out.

"They're stopping to sleep at night because they do not know we are trying to catch them. How much sleep have we had? A short rest at Sheep Camp and Caribou Crossing," Split the Waves continued, trying to relieve his friend's worries as they powered downriver.

"Speaking of sleep," Julianna interjected, "the mosquitoes were biting me so badly that I did not fall asleep until just before you woke me. Could I sleep in the boat? I will be useless if I don't catch an hour of shut-eye. And could you please stop arguing?"

"Do you want us to sing you a bedtime song?" Salkusta asked with good humour. "Split the Waves has a tune he sings about a wanderer always searching for his love. But it is a sad tale, because in the end the wanderer dies, but he has joined his loved one."

Julianna could not imagine why she thought this song was familiar. Maybe it was her sleep-deprived brain that made today's events seem as if they had occurred to her before.

"Please sing to me, Split the Waves," Julianna murmured, as she curled up in the bottom of the boat, resting comfortably on the packs and listening to Split the Waves sing a strange Tlingit melody. It seemed as if she had just closed her eyes when Split the Waves woke her.

"Time to paddle, River Woman." He shook her gently. "Salkusta has to sleep. He thinks he sees the *Devil's Own* every time a log floats by. Soon, he will be seeing Katu in the canoe with him."

"That would be a beautiful sight," Salkusta added. "Maybe I will dream of her while you two paddle me across Lake Laberge. Are you stopping to eat at Jim Boss Town, or do you go farther?"

"Go to sleep, Salkusta. We are not stopping till we cross the lake. And his name is Kishwoot, meaning 'Pound the Table.' He is chief of the Ta'an people. This lake is his territory. When the Klondikers entered Lake Laberge this year, he tried to charge them for crossing his lake. He is the kind of chief we need to keep these newcomers from running over us."

Salkusta was too tired, and Julianna too puzzled to speak. *Jim Boss,* she thought, *where have I heard that name before?"*

They paddled into the night. It was a warm June evening, with no wind. The slanting rays of the sun coloured the water pink and gold. As the sun dipped below the horizon for the short June night, a pale moon rose, trying to compete with the setting sun. A blaze of colour washed over the mountains and reflected across the lake. The water splashing from her paddle looked like melted gold. Julianna felt she was on a magical journey.

The boat sped along the cliffs of Lake Laberge, first in the half-light and then into the morning sun. Salkusta woke to take over the paddling and let Split the Waves sleep for a couple of hours. Ahead, Julianna could see the end of the lake. Somewhere there was an outlet and Thirty Mile, the fastest section of the Yukon River.

"Where's the river?" Julianna whispered to Salkusta.

"See that valley coming in at the end of the lake where the trees are a lighter green?" Split the Waves answered, waking up and peering ahead at the far shore. "Maybe we should stop at Lower Laberge for breakfast. We can buy hot coffee and bread there."

"Are you sure? I think I have been to Lower Laberge before, and there were only a few abandoned buildings."

"Jim Boss's family sells food there, and the Mounties have a post. Maybe someone can tell us when Crump passed through."

They found the outlet to the river. At first the current was poky, but then they were speeding along, relieved to be in fast water again and having a break from the long lake crossing.

Before long, they reached Lower Laberge, previously a native fishing site. Now the North-West Mounted Police were established here, checking the Klondikers as they passed into Thirty Mile. Julianna stumbled onto the shore, her legs feeling shaky and almost giving away beneath her. She began to walk towards the Mounted Police headquarters when Split the Waves caught up to her.

"You maybe want to wait at the boat."

"Why? I want to ask them about my family," Julianna replied.

Split the Waves didn't want to continue. He paused, then carried on. "They will be very rude to you because they will think you are my wife, and they look down on a white woman who marries into the Indian tribes. I don't want you to be hurt. I will ask them about your family and find out when Crump passed by. The Mounted Police know about Soapy Smith's gang and don't want them to set up their scam games here in our country. They will help us find Crump."

Julianna returned to the boat, where Salkusta was getting out some food.

"Now, River Woman, you're upset about something."

"I feel bad because your people are mistreated even though this is your country. I would like to be part of Split the Waves' family, but I don't want to be treated like dirt."

"It not good what happens to us, but what can we do? Maybe just try and get rich like Split the Waves. He ignores the bad people's remarks and figures out how to live in their world better than the white people. Now he comes with news about Crump, right?"

Split the Waves ran back to the boat, "They're only a day ahead of us! The *Devil's Own* passed by this time yesterday."

"We catch him soon! I bet he stop at Little Salmon and Fort Selkirk," Salkusta added with excitement.

"What about my family?" Julianna asked. Split the Waves shook his head.

They pushed off from shore. Salkusta was energized from the good news and paddled at a pace that sent streams of perspiration down his round face. The current remained fast and the little group sped on past Hootalinqua and later that day reached Big Salmon Village. Both settlements had North-West Mounted Police stations. Many of the Klondikers stopped at these river points to spend the night in comfort, visiting with fellow travellers. Julianna and her two companions were determined to catch Crump before he reached Dawson. They kept paddling all through the night and into the next day.

By mid-day, the sun was burning down on them. Julianna dipped a scarf in the water and draped it over her head to try and keep from getting over-heated. It was a blisteringly hot day as they approached Five Finger Rapids, the last obstacle on their long journey. Julianna almost wished they would flip in the rapids just so she could cool down. They had taken turns napping on the way from Little Salmon Village to Five Fingers but were becoming fatigued.

"Look!" she screamed. "There's a polar bear! Paddle! He's after us!"

"What are you yelling about? There are no polar bears on the Yukon River," said Split the Waves.

"But it was coming right at us," Julianna insisted. "Didn't you see it?"

"No, I didn't," Split the Waves answered. "Salkusta, did you see a polar bear?"

"No, but I just saw a raven as big as the sky. It was calling me and saying, 'Hurry. Hurry. Paddle faster. They just ahead.' Then it grew so big that it blocked the sun, and everything went black for a minute. I guess my mind is going," Salkusta admitted.

"But Split the Waves has not been hallucinating, have you?" Julianna asked.

"Well, I have to admit I thought the boat was full of squirrels and they were all chirping at me," Split the Waves answered. "I knew there couldn't be squirrels in the boat, so I didn't say anything. I was worried that you would think I was crazy."

"We are all crazy," Julianna admitted. "When will we get to sleep again? I'm so weary that I fell asleep for a minute and almost dropped my paddle in the water."

"Just don't sleep when we go through Five Fingers," Split the Waves warned. "The warm weather has made the river high, so it will not be the usual easy run."

"I think I see the rocky towers up ahead. We have to go right, right?" Julianna laughed giddily.

"Right, go right," Split the Waves chanted. "Salkusta, keep the boat going straight, and Julianna and I will keep up the speed."

The sentinels of Five Fingers loomed ahead. The river seemed so quiet, without even a ripple, yet they could hear the roar of the water as it choked through the narrow passages ahead. They veered into the chute to their right. The water boiled against the mid-river rock towers. They sped through, bouncing up one wave and down the other. The bow dipped into the oncoming waves, completely submerging Salkusta. But the boat surfaced, and they were through, slipping along in the downstream ripples.

"What's that?" Salkusta yelled over the roar of the rapids. The boat passed several pieces of gear floating about in the eddy below the rapids. "I guess one of the Klondikers tipped," Split the Waves answered.

"Look, there they are!" Just ahead, two people were trying to swim for shore. Julianna and Split the Waves steered the canoe towards the swimmers, who were floundering in the swift current. They pulled alongside the men.

"Hold onto the boat. One of you on each side," Split the Waves yelled. The exhausted men grabbed onto the gunnels. Salkusta pulled into an eddy, and the two strangers staggered onto the shore. One was over six feet in height, with thick arms and an immense chest. The other was younger, not much older than Split the Waves, but heavy-set like his companion.

"Are you okay?" Julianna asked.

"Thanks, ma'am. You saved our lives. We couldn't get out of the current. It was too swift. Thank you all," the older of the two said in an exhausted voice.

"Where's Crump?" the younger man yelled, looking downriver.

"I saw that filth leave. I bet he ditched us so he don't have to pay our wages," the older man grumbled.

"Did you say Crump?" Salkusta asked. "Were you guys on his boat, the *Devil's Own?*"

"We wished we weren't. We lost our gear just out of Lindeman. Gaston, here, was sure we could run the river, and we got tipped over in the fast water," said the younger man, indicating that he was talking about his companion, the burly boat-man. "Lost everything, so when Crump came along, well, we joined up with him as boat-men. So what does he do? When the boat tips, he hangs on and goes to shore with it. Does he try and rescue us? No way! He hops in, pulls out the oars and leaves us to drown. He's in trouble, not just with us, but he won't get his woman now because he doesn't have the blankets and year of food he has to pay."

"What about the five thousand?" Salkusta couldn't resist asking. "Did it go down with the gear?"

"He was lucky there," the younger man replied. "Crump kept his dough in a belt around his waist. I'd like to get hold of him now. That money would be mine if I could catch him."

"We want to catch him, too," Julianna said. "Maybe we could take you along."

"River Woman, can I talk to you?" Split the Waves said, walking away from the others.

"These fellows were Crump's men. How do you know they aren't still in cahoots with him, and why should we take them when it will just slow us down?"

"I don't know. I just had a feeling that they would help us. Do you think that it was wrong to offer them a ride?"

"Well, I guess it's too late now," Split the Waves said. "They're already getting into our boat and settling in. I just hope your second sense is correct."

They moved much slower now that the boat was encumbered by two more men, especially big heavy men weighing twice as much as Julianna. As they paddled along, they recovered several packs that had fallen out of the *Devil's Own.*

"Hey, look at this," the young boat-man yelled. "It's the wedding dress for Crump's woman!"

"Hey, Kid," Gaston cautioned, "I don't think they like the idea of one of their young women marrying a mean, ugly guy like Crump, so keep your trap shut."

"You're right about that, you two," Julianna added.

Salkusta scowled and doubled his efforts at paddling. There was little talk as the tired paddlers kept up their pace for the next hour.

"The Kid and I can take over," Gaston offered. "You must be worn to the bone if you paddled all the way from Lake Laberge without camping. How do you do it? I am supposed to be the best on the river, and the fastest trip I've made from Lake Laberge to Fort Selkirk is three days, and you kids will do it in just over a day."

"Okay, you two paddle, but Salkusta will paddle with you," Split the Waves said. *And keep an eye on you*, he said to himself.

"Pull over to that old cabin, and we'll switch positions."

When they landed on shore, a man stumbled out of the broken-down shack. "Help!" he cried. "We're starving and my wife is so ill she's out of her mind."

Julianna was the first to get to the cabin. A woman in her thirties lay on a dirty cot, moaning in pain. Julianna put her hand on the woman's feverish forehead, noticing her blistered lips and discoloured skin. Julianna had never seen anyone look so ill and had no idea what was wrong.

Split the Waves looked at the woman. "She has scurvy. It's the food they eat. Just beans and more beans. No meat and no berries for months."

"What can we do for her?" Julianna asked, concerned for this unfortunate victim of the gold rush.

"Could you fetch the food bag, Salkusta?" Split the Waves asked. "I brought a few oranges back from Dyea. I was hoping to give them to my cousins in Alsek, but I think she needs them more."

Salkusta opened the food bag and dug out an orange. "Maybe she should only have the juice. What you think, Split the Waves?"

Split the Waves nodded in agreement. "Squeeze the orange and mix the juice with a little warm water."

The woman's husband tried to help with the fire but was too weak to be of any assistance. Salkusta guided him to a chair.

"You rest now. We make some hot water for your woman and then I give you some soup. Is that okay? What do we call you?" Salkusta asked.

"Joe's the name. I come from Ohio. If only we can get back to that warm place with fields of potatoes, I won't care if we are poor," he sighed.

Without being asked, Gaston and the Kid made a blazing fire in the pit outside the cabin and soon had the kettle boiling. There were more helpers than victims. Everyone pitched in. The Kid brought soft fir boughs to make a bed for the sick man, then cleaned up the small cabin.

"The water must not be too hot," Split the Waves cautioned. "Just mix half and half water and orange juice and maybe a little sugar, and we will see if she can drink it."

Julianna tried to offer the woman a drink, speaking gently to her and supporting her back. Instead of being thankful, the ill woman looked angrily at Julianna, cursed her and knocked the cup to the floor.

Julianna jumped up. "What's wrong with her?"

The defeated-looking husband watched this performance and staggered over to his wife. "Anna, please don't fight and take your drink. They're trying to help."

Anna burst into tears, her thin body shaking in violent sobs.

"Come now, that's okay." Her husband held another cup of juice to her lips. This time, she accepted the drink and fell back on the bed exhausted.

Gaston cut more wood and piled it high in a sheltered spot beside the cabin, leaving Salkusta, Split the Waves and Julianna free to care for the sick Klondikers. Salkusta brought warm soup to the thin, worn-out man, who was now resting comfortably.

"Ah, that's the first food I've had for a week," the man said gratefully. "It tastes like the best meal I've ever eaten, and it's just a bowl of soup. You've saved me, but tell me, will Anna make it? She hasn't been right in her mind and will not even help to save herself."

"She has scurvy very bad. That could be causing her craziness," Split the Waves answered in a soft voice. "I see your people die of this last year when they spend their first winter in the gold fields. You need to eat the sap from the spruce trees when you have no greens and no berries. I'll give you my other two oranges. Make sure she eats everything in the orange, first the juice, then the pulp and also the skin. Maybe she can only drink the juice until she's better. Then I leave you with some pemmican. It's made of berries and fat and dried meat. That will keep you from getting scurvy too, and I hope it will make your woman well. She can't travel for a long time though, because she is too weak."

"We can't continue anyway. We were trying to get out of the Klondike by going upriver and then across the pass to Skagway. We were told it wouldn't be too hard because your people pole upriver all the time. We did not expect the water to be so high. It took all our strength to make it this far. Anna has always been the sweetest wife to me, but not on this trip. She did not eat or drink water, and when exhaustion overtook her, she became a different person. She screamed at me like a madwoman, calling me names that the worst criminal would use. I can't bear to hear her like that again. I would rather drown in Five Fingers." He sighed with the deep sorrow of a defeated man.

"How did you lose your belongings?" Julianna asked.

"The boat tipped when the water rose so high. We lost everything, even the gold I mined last winter. We took shelter in this cabin, but Anna became frantic if I left her side. I couldn't even go down to the water's edge to call for help. Then I was too weak to go. God must have sent you just in time."

"I wish we could help you more, but we have to go to Fort Selkirk tonight," Salkusta said. "If we don't leave soon, I may as well die."

"We will catch up with Crump," Split the Waves said, "but we have to make sure these people don't die. Your woman needs to go to the hospital. She will not be able to pole upstream for even a mile, let alone three hundred miles and until she recovers, she cannot climb over the Chilkoot Trail."

"I'd go back to Dawson in a minute," the man said, "but how?"

"We fix you a raft in no time," Gaston said, joining the group in the small cabin. "I've already cut the logs. With four men to work, we can finish the job while you pack your things."

"Four men and a woman," Julianna corrected. "What makes you think I can't help build the raft?"

"Not again," Gaston answered with a chuckle. "Every woman I meet calls me out for treating them like a woman. Sure, I bet you can hit a nail on the head every time."

"Well," Julianna admitted, "that's not my strong suit. But I can fetch the logs while you pound."

They worked hard, not pausing until the raft was set in the river and packed for the trip. They had built a bed for Anna, sheltered from the sun. Already, her husband's energy had returned, and he was able to help load the raft.

"Gaston, Salkusta has to catch up to Crump," Split the Waves said. "Could you take Joe and Anna on the raft? We have to paddle fast, and the raft will slow us down."

"Just as long as you punch Crump's ugly nose for me and git our wages back for us," Gaston replied.

Gaston and the Kid carried Anna to her sheltered bed and boarded the raft with Joe. Julianna, Salkusta and Split the Waves returned to their canoe to paddle for Dawson. Gaston and the Kid poled the raft into the river, heading downstream, also back to Dawson where Joe could try to make back his lost gold poke, and Anna could be taken to the hospital to cure her soul as well as her ravaged body.

Once back in the current, Salkusta paddled at a pace that exhausted his companions. The lost time was weighing on his mind, and although he did not speak of it, Julianna and Split the Waves were aware of his concern. Salkusta thought that Crump had already reached Dawson and was claiming Katu that day.

Split the Waves and Julianna took turns paddling and then resting. Salkusta wouldn't stop and wouldn't rest. He was focused on reaching Fort Selkirk before morning. The midnight sun made it possible to paddle or drift through the night, but the strain of the long hours was wearing on the three young people. After a hot day, the weather changed and a strong wind wailed at them. The paddlers were exhausted from lack of sleep and food.

Julianna often reminded her companions to drink water and take snacks of dried salmon. "Remember, if you don't look after yourselves, you may lose your mind like Anna and swear at me."

"Even if I was completely insane, I would never speak angry words to you," Split the Waves responded. "Anyway, soon we'll have a rest at Fort Selkirk."

"Where is that place?" Julianna asked, frustrated that it was taking so long.

"When you see the high banks with the hole on the cliff, you know you are just about at Fort Selkirk," Split the Waves informed her.

"We'd better speed up," Salkusta suggested, "or we may miss Crump."

There was no rest for the weary young people. Although they had no sleep for over a day, they paddled the remaining stretch into Fort Selkirk without a break. Finally, Julianna spotted the banks of the Pelly River and the fortress-like cliffs. It was late evening and the Fort was quiet as they paddled to shore and tied up beside a flotilla of river boats. Salkusta jumped out.

"It's here!" he exclaimed. "The *Devil's Own* is here!" Salkusta was so excited that he could not keep his voice down.

"Let's not wake up the entire town," Split the Waves cautioned. "We don't need to beat up Crump. We'll just do a little job on his boat." Split the Waves took an axe from the dug-out and sliced a good-sized hole in the *Devil's Own*. "There, that should stop him. Now I suggest we go downriver and find Katu."

But Salkusta wouldn't leave without meeting his enemy face to face. He had chased the swindler for days, packing over the mountain pass and canoeing for endless hours without sleep. Now he had to confront this evil man. Despite Julianna's pleas, Salkusta crept up to the settlement. He was in luck, for in the light of the June evening Salkusta could see someone sneaking around the outside of the Hudson's Bay store, first trying one window, then another. He knew it was Crump from the description they had been given. Salkusta spotted the gold watch hanging across the villain's bulging stomach. Crump was the picture of evil. Salkusta hid behind a tree and watched. Crump jimmied open a window and disappeared into the store. Salkusta ran back to the boat, calling to Julianna and Split the Waves.

"I saw him! He broke into the store. He's stealing to get the stuff he lost in the river. We just need to bring the police, and they'll catch him…how do you say it?"

"Red-handed," Julianna added.

"Come, Split the Waves! You talk to the Mounties! You know where they have their station."

Salkusta and Split the Waves ran up the riverbank. Suddenly alone, Julianna felt uneasy at being separated, but they were out of her sight before she could warn them to be careful. She remained with the boat while Salkusta and Split the Waves headed for the North-West Mounted Police barracks.

"Look!" Salkusta shouted. "He dropped one of the blankets."

"Don't touch it!" Split the Waves yelled. But the warning came too late. Salkusta was holding the blanket when the store manager burst out of his house holding a rifle.

"I saw you sneaking in my store and now I have you with the goods," the angry man yelled.

Split the Waves was so shocked he could only stutter. "Bu–but…"

Salkusta tried to explain. "Your store was robbed by Crump. I have to catch him." Salkusta ran towards the boats. The store owner lowered the gun and fired. Salkusta fell to the ground, screaming in pain and holding his leg.

"Don't you try anything," the store owner yelled at Split the Waves, "or you will get the same."

Two Mounties ran from the barracks with pistols raised.

"What's going on here?"

"I caught these two thieves with one of the store blankets. See, here's the evidence," the store manager said. "They probably took much more, and I'll make sure I get everything back. No one steals from the Hudson's Bay and gets away with it."

"We'll look after them," the officer said. "Raise your hands in the air," he ordered Split the Waves, "and you get up," he yelled at Salkusta. "That bullet just grazed you."

The two young men were marched to the station and locked up.

When Julianna heard the gunshot, she started up the bank. Blocking her path was the ugliest and meanest-looking man she had ever encountered. He was dragging two huge packs filled with supplies. In the other hand was a pistol aimed at Julianna's chest. She knew it was Crump.

"Don't move another inch," he growled. "You and me are going downriver in your boyfriend's boat."

CHAPTER 12

KIDNAPPED

Julianna trembled as she stepped into the canoe, keeping her eyes on the gun.

"Now let's see if you can paddle," Crump yelled. "I want to reach the Klondike in two days and no more, so let's keep up a good pace, just like you and your boyfriends."

"They did all the paddling," Julianna lied. "I just sat in the canoe resting and passing them food and water."

Julianna picked up the paddle but did not put any effort into her stroke. She barely pushed any water against the blade and her pace slowed to a crawl.

"You're the weakest paddler I've ever had to put up with. Use some muscle or it will take us a week to make the Klondike."

"I'm not used to this," Julianna said. "Maybe it would be better if you paddled on your own and I rested."

"Maybe I should throw you overboard," Crump grumbled. "Now git working. At least I can sell you to Skeeter, a real crook, so he can make a few dollars off your useless flesh."

"No one sells me. I have family, and they will see you rot in jail for this," Julianna yelled back defiantly.

"If you had a family they wouldn't let you hook up with Indians. No proper man will have anything to do with you now so you may as well throw in with the likes of me."

"You're just making up stories so I can be forced to work for your wicked friends," Julianna answered, burning with indignation.

"We'll see. You'll come around when you realize your boyfriends will be in jail for the next ten years and you have nowhere to sleep and nothing to eat," Crump continued.

"They're innocent and you know it," Julianna yelled back at Crump, her face red with anger. "I'll go to the police and tell them about you."

"You won't get the chance, cause after we pick up Katu, we will be heading out of Canada and away from the Mounties. So git used to my company. Now let's see you put some effort into moving this here canoe."

Julianna moved the paddle through the water, still pretending that she was unfamiliar with a canoe and was a hopeless paddler.

"If the police have Salkusta and Split the Waves, will they keep them at Fort Selkirk?" Julianna asked.

"Nah, they'll go to trial in Klondike, or what they call Dawson. Your Indian friends don't have a chance. They'll be guilty before they even get to the court. No one will take the word of a couple of Indian guys over the testimony of the Hudson's Bay. Even if you showed up at court, they wouldn't take the word of a Indian's white squaw," Crump chuckled with an evil, sickly laugh. "So we'll just forget about them. No one to rescue Katu, and no one to save you."

Julianna realized that Crump was right. She could not keep back the tears, thinking that she would never find her family; maybe they had left the country without her. She would never see Split the Waves again and Salkusta would likely kill himself if Katu was taken by this filthy old man. *How could this happen when they had tried so hard?*

They made slow progress towards Dawson. The river braided, and Julianna purposely steered the boat into the slowest channel. Another time, she was able to lodge the boat in the shallow water and would not get out to help Crump pull the boat off the gravel bar. She often glanced downstream, hoping to see the police boat that would carry Salkusta and Split the Waves to Dawson.

Julianna calculated the time it would take for the Mounties to get ready and bring Salkusta and Split the Waves into town. She also wondered if Gaston and the Kid would be able to catch up to them, even on the slow raft.

Back at Fort Selkirk, little progress was made towards the trip to Dawson. The Mounties arranged for a nurse to dress Salkusta's wound and spent time questioning the two young men. Split the Waves and Salkusta did not say much to the Mounties, believing that no matter what they said, their side of the story would not be heard. Salkusta lay on the bunk in the jailhouse, dejected and silent.

"At least try and help me find a way to escape," Split the Waves urged. "If we do not get out of here today, we will be taken to Klondike, and they will put us in jail until we are old men and Katu has ten children from Crump."

This was too much for Salkusta. He leapt from his cot and rushed at Split the Waves, tears in his eyes. "Do not say that! Do not think that! She will kill herself before she marry that old man. She my woman." He grabbed Split the Waves around the throat, choking him and sobbing in anguish.

Split the Waves pulled Salkusta's hands off his throat and instead of fighting back, Split the Waves put his arms around his distraught friend.

"I am so sorry," he said, patting Salkusta and holding him. "It is all my fault. I promised we would catch Crump. But please, Salkusta, we must not give up. My friend has been taken, too. Remember what River Woman told us. We must try to save our loved one until there is no breath left in our bodies."

Salkusta was still shaking with emotions but was no longer angry. He was quiet for a minute, remembering Julianna's words.

"Yes, we must, and maybe I have an idea," Salkusta said. He banged his wounded leg against the bunk over and over until the bandages were soaked with blood, letting out cries of pain that could be heard across the settlement. In minutes the door opened, and one of the Mounties stood with a pistol ready.

"I need the doctor in Klondike," Salkusta said. "You have to take me right now, or I die from loss of blood."

The policeman looked at Salkusta's leg and saw the blood seep from his bandaged leg.

"We were going to take you tomorrow, but we also have a sick woman who needs to go to the hospital. I guess we will take you boys and her together."

"It's Anna, isn't it?" Split the Waves asked. "Her husband will tell you we helped them, and Gaston and the Kid know that Crump is a thief. Ask them," Split the Waves insisted. "They'll tell you we're innocent."

"I'll question them," the policeman replied, "but the Hudson's Bay store owner insists you go to court. So, we all go to court and hear each person's story. I can't let you go, but I promise you will get a fair hearing."

The Mounties found Gaston and the Kid at breakfast, enjoying a plate of beans and fried potatoes. The two river men concentrated on their meal. They slurped their food, their mouths close to their bowls, shovelling their breakfast in with huge spoonfuls, to be washed down with coffee.

"Let's hear your side of this," one of the Mounties said.

Gaston wiped his mouth with his sleeve before he related the story of their rescue at Five Fingers. He confirmed everything the young Indian men had said. He then went on to describe the raft journey to Fort Selkirk.

"The trip downriver was hell, pure living hell. This woman here, the sick one, never slept. She was frightened by every log in the river and every bit of shallow water. She was screaming at me all the way. 'Can't you see that log, you dumb ass! Get some glasses! We're going to hit it! Go right, I tell you.' Then, if I didn't do what she wanted, it would be another blast of profanity. Worse words than I have ever heard. I can't even repeat the names she called me. Joe tried to calm her down and get her to sleep a wink or two, but she wouldn't close her eyes. I guess she thought I was going to drown her if she didn't keep watch on every turn of the river. Me, Gaston, who is known to be the best river man in the country. Her life was saved by them young Indians and the girl, but she never even thanked them."

"Do you swear that the Indian boys are innocent?" the officer questioned.

"They're telling the truth." It was Joe who had listened to Gaston while he stood at the kitchen door. "I'm sorry to hear that my Anna caused so much trouble. She didn't know what she was doing. But it won't do any good if you let Crump get away. At least let Gaston and the Kid go downriver and catch up with that thief."

"I know you have a good reputation as a hard worker and a strong paddler," the Mountie said to Gaston, "but you have an equally bad reputation for getting boozed up and falling in with the worst cheaters in the Klondike."

"He was a good man when he was with us," Joe confirmed.

With this testimony, the Mounties decided to give Gaston and the Kid a boat and let them chase after Crump. The factor's wife gave Anna a cool room to rest in and prepared a meal for the sick couple. As long as Anna was away from the river, she felt safe and was calm and co-operative.

It was several hours before the Mounties loaded up their boat and helped Joe carry Anna down to the water. The Mounties were aware of the sick woman's fear of the river and had given her laudanum, a potent drug, to calm her for the trip to Dawson. They tied Split the Waves' and Salkusta's hands behind their backs and made them sit in the middle of the canoe beside Anna and Joe.

"I feel very bad for you two boys," Joe explained to Split the Waves and Salkusta. "You were good to us and look what happens to you." Then he turned to the constable and tried once more to convince the Mounties that Split the Waves and Salkusta could not have been the thieves.

As they travelled downriver, Joe was able to convince the Mounties that the guilty man was getting away and that Split the Waves and Salkusta were innocent.

"If you believe Joe, why not let us go?" Split the Waves argued. "At least let us paddle. Salkusta and I could make this boat go twice as fast because we must speed to save our loved ones."

"Okay, boys, take over the paddling. But don't try and jump overboard. We will see you get a fair trial even if it is in front of a white man's judge."

They untied Split the Waves and Salkusta, and the two young men took over the paddling. Immediately, the canoe picked up speed. They chose the fastest channel and never let up the pace. They knew that Crump had likely reached Dawson, but they hoped he could be caught before getting away with Katu and River Woman.

Gaston and the Kid were hours ahead, paddling fast. Julianna saw a boat approaching and hoped that the speck in the distance was the Mounties' boat, carrying Split the Waves and Salkusta. She slowed her pace and pretended to fall asleep.

"Hey you! Git paddling or I'll sell you to the worst of the miners in Fort Yukon. I know a sixty-year-old guy that will pay lots of gold for you. He is so ugly even his mother couldn't love him."

Julianna ignored these warnings, yawned and pretended her arms were aching. She took a few strokes and then stopped. "Could we stop for a drink? See that fresh stream? I would paddle much better if I could just have a drink of fresh water."

Crump believed the story and pulled over to the bank. Julianna went into the bushes, taking her time. When she returned to the bank, the approaching boat was in full view. It was not the Mounties. It was Gaston and the Kid.

They sped towards shore and were met by Crump pointing a gun at Gaston.

"What's this, Crump?" Gaston asked. "We have no hard feelings about being dumped in the river. Look, we have a good boat and had no problem catching up with you. Let's hook up, and we can go into Dawson together. I see you got yourself a pretty woman. Took the Indian's squaw, did you?"

At these words, Julianna burned with anger. *How could they pretend they were on my side, that they hated Crump? It was all lies.* She felt stupid for believing that Gaston and the Kid were good men.

"How could you betray us after we saved your worthless lives?" Julianna yelled, as Gaston and the Kid pulled their boat to shore. "Why don't the two of you go to Dawson and swindle innocent people until you get caught? And to think I was taken in by you!"

Julianna stomped off when she realized that she was not being rescued by Gaston and the Kid. Instead, she felt betrayed.

"Don't try anything smart with me, Gaston," Crump said. "Okay, I know I left you and the Kid at Five Fingers, but I'll pay your wages. Just help me git to Dawson."

"There's food here, woman with the wicked tongue," the Kid called.

"I wouldn't eat with you snakes if I had no food for a month."

Julianna walked down the gravel beach, hoping that somehow Split the Waves would be able to rescue her. She kept glancing upriver. There were many rafts, scows and even the occasional small steamer on the river but the Mounties' boat was not in sight. She wanted to scream for help, but the boats all passed by on the far side of the river beyond hearing distance. Besides, Crump kept his pistol close by, and Julianna understood that he would not have any qualms about using it.

Despite the warm day, Gaston built a fire and was brewing tea when she returned.

"Have a cup of tea," Gaston offered. "It is still a long way into Dawson City."

Crump seemed anxious to leave, but again, Gaston took his time loading up the gear.

"Do we leave the girl behind?" Gaston asked Crump.

"I was going to take her to Fort Yukon where she may bring a good price, but I think she may be more trouble than she's worth. We'll leave her behind, but make sure she can't call for help. Hey Kid! Take her up into the hills and tie her up. No one will find her out here," Crump ordered. "You can take Gaston's boat and meet us in Dawson."

"Let's go, River Woman," the Kid ordered. The husky young man grabbed Julianna's arm and pulled her away from the campsite. Julianna kicked at the Kid, convinced they were in with Crump.

"Your mother will never forgive you if you do such a wicked deed," Julianna said.

"I am not going to do anything to you," the Kid whispered once they were far enough away from Crump. "If you would just stop kicking me, it would give me a chance to explain that Gaston is trying to rescue you. He is doing everything to slow Crump down in the hope that the police will catch up with him when they come downriver with Split the Waves and Salkusta."

"I don't believe you," Julianna said stubbornly. "I only trust Split the Waves."

"Well don't trust me, but I can tell you that I am to keep you until Crump and Gaston take off downriver, then we will wait till the police show up and get them to go after Crump."

"You're lying like you always do. I'll get Crump myself!" Julianna delivered a sharp kick at the Kid and ran back to the camp.

Before Crump could stop her, Julianna pushed the heavily loaded dug-out into the current.

"Now you won't have the fifty blankets and year's supply of food, you dirty old man," she yelled at Crump, "and you won't ever get Katu."

The boat was drifting downriver when Julianna waded out with the second boat, trying to push it into the current.

"Go after her!" Crump ordered. Gaston did not move.

Crump swore at Gaston and plunged into the water pulling the boat and Julianna back to shore. He flung the young girl onto the gravel beach.

"Now you will git in the boat and paddle like the devil," he yelled at Julianna. "And I know what you two have been up to." He turned angrily to Gaston and the Kid. "You have been working against me. A fire on the hottest day of summer? Tea, when the last thing you would want is a hot drink. Gittin' the Kid to tie up the woman? Do you think I was born yesterday?" Crump's face, normally puffy and distorted, now turned blue with anger.

He placed the pistol against Julianna's neck. "So, you want to save her life," he said to Gaston and the Kid, "I'll tell you what you can do. The two of you head into the bush and I want to see ya at the top of that hill waving a kerchief at me and I want to hear ya blowing that whistle. If I don't see and hear ya by the time we git down to that bend in the river, the girl will have a bullet through her head. Now git!"

Julianna could feel the cold steel against her neck. "I think you better do as he says," she told them. "I am sorry I didn't believe you, Kid. I guess you were trying to help me."

Gaston and the Kid took off through the bushes and disappeared. Julianna was once more alone with her dangerous captor. Again, she pretended she couldn't paddle, but Crump bellowed at her to use her muscle and wouldn't stop yelling until she paddled hard.

"Catch up to the dug-out, you little witch!"

Julianna feared for her life and did what her kidnapper demanded. As they approached the bend, Crump and Julianna looked up on the hill. Gaston and the Kid were not in sight. Julianna turned to look at Crump and gasped. He held the pistol in his hands, pointed directly at her back. A shot rang out, reverberating through the river valley.

Gaston and the Kid were not quite at the top of the hill when they heard the gun fire. They were stunned.

"My God! He's shot her!" Gaston yelled. "He didn't even wait until he reached the bend!"

"How could he kill someone that young and a girl to boot? What did she ever do to him to deserve to die?" the Kid lamented.

At the top of the hill, Gaston waved the kerchief, and the Kid blew his whistle in panic.

As they made their way down to the river, they blamed themselves for not protecting the young girl. Then, approaching the camp, they saw a boat. It was only a speck. As the boat came closer, Gaston recognized the distinctive North-West Mounted Police boat and was able to make out that Split the Waves and Salkusta were the paddlers. Gaston and the Kid began running through the thick brush but realized they would never reach the river before the boat passed.

"Your whistle!" Gaston yelled anxiously.

The Kid blew repeated blasts on the whistle. The surrounding hills caught sound like an opera house, and the men in the boat could clearly hear the distress call. They looked around and spotted Gaston, frantically waving his kerchief. The two abandoned men were out on the bank when the Mounties and their charges landed.

"So now do you yellow legs believe that Crump is the real criminal?" Gaston demanded of the two Mounties. Gaston told his story, but could not bring himself to tell Split the Waves that he feared that River Woman had been shot.

"Maybe, if you would be more respectful," one of the officers said.

"Did you not know that everyone calls you 'yellow legs' because of the stripe down the pants? It isn't meant as disrespect. It is just what you are called."

"Call me Constable McKenzie, and maybe I will check out the story. You say that the stolen goods will be given to an Indian man named Harold in trade for his niece Katu. And you, Salkusta, are you familiar with this man Harold?"

"I can show you where he stays," Salkusta answered, "but we must lose no time. He may already have Katu, and we have to save her."

"Is River Woman okay?" Split the Waves asked.

"Crump took her downriver," Gaston said, his voice shaking, then added, "I can't tell you if she is unharmed. He's so crazy, that man."

"What do you know about this?" Split the Waves yelled, aware there was more to the story than Gaston was letting on.

"We heard the gun go off. Crump threatened to kill her, but we don't know what happened," Gaston answered reluctantly.

"He told us to wave a kerchief to let him know we were on top of the hill. We are big and slow and can't run up a hill that fast. He didn't wait," the Kid added, dejectedly.

Split the Waves listened to the dreadful account of his beloved friend. He said nothing but was inwardly tortured by feelings of guilt over not protecting River Woman.

"You don't know she is dead," Salkusta reasoned. "We must go after him. She may only be hurt and needs us, and we must try and save her and Katu."

The Kid and Gaston helped with the paddling. Split the Waves and Salkusta could not rest and with six men at the paddles, the boat sped towards Dawson. Gaston, with his tremendous strength, was able to paddle two strokes to their one and soon they rounded the bend and saw the big scar on the hillside, which the native people called "Moosehide." This scar was the signal that Dawson City was only minutes downriver.

"Let's be lively now boys. We're coming to the Klondike, and you need to guide Constable Winters and me to Harold's," Constable McKenzie said to Salkusta.

CHAPTER 13

THE KLONDIKE

The bullet was so close that Julianna could feel it whistle past her head. Her heart pounding, she dug her paddle into the water, terrified that the next shot would find its mark. As they approached the bend in the river, both Julianna and Crump tried to spot Gaston and the Kid. There was no sign of them. *Now I'll be killed for sure!* Julianna thought.

"See how little they care for you. They won't even run up the hill to save you." Crump picked up the pistol once again.

"Help!" she cried. But there was no one to hear her frantic cry.

His finger was on the trigger when the shrill whistle echoed across the river. Julianna looked up the hill. There, in the distance, she could see the white kerchief being waved. She was spared!

"Don't think you are free to lily paddle. I want some muscle behind your stroke," Crump demanded.

Julianna was exhausted from her close encounter with death, but she was afraid that Crump would carry out his threats if she didn't paddle. Ahead, she could see the dug-out drifting slowly towards Dawson. Soon, they caught the boat. Crump told her to pull it to shore, where they left Gaston's boat, and they got back in the big dug-out with the supply of blankets and food. This was the payment Crump would make for Katu.

Julianna could not think of what she could do to either save herself or the doomed Han girl. Tears of exhaustion and frustration began to roll down her cheeks. She had been racing for days, covering a thousand kilometres from Dyea, only to have Crump win in the end. *How could they have failed? What will Salkusta do if he loses Katu?* Julianna sobbed quietly as they approached the gold rush city.

If she had been a Klondiker, she would have been ecstatic at the first signs of the Klondike. Instead, her heart was heavy when she spotted the haphazard collection of tents and new buildings crowded on the riverbank. This place was Lousetown, at the confluence of the Klondike and Yukon rivers. Just ahead, the fast waters of the Klondike River flowed in from the valley on her right. Before they reached the river, Crump ordered her to pull into an eddy where he tied up the boat.

"I'm paying a quick business visit to Katu's uncle in Lousetown, and since you are not to be trusted, I'll just have to tie you up while I pick up my bride." Crump voice was like steel grating across gravel.

"She will never be your wife! She is promised to Salkusta, and he will slit your throat as soon as he catches you," Julianna declared.

"He'll never catch me. I saw the police put Split the Waves and Salkusta into the slammer, charged with taking these here supplies. Do you think the judge is going to believe a couple of Indian boys? I don't think so. They'll probably try to escape because they know they'll be found guilty and when they run from the Mounties, they'll both git what's coming to them—a bullet through the heart because the Mounties know how to shoot. Which is why I'm leaving the Klondike. Too many lawmen here. You and me and Katu will go where a guy like me can have a young squaw for a bride and can sell young girls for a good price with no questions asked. In the States, we make our own laws. Git out now and put your hands behind your back," Crump ordered.

He tied Julianna's hands and secured her to a tree, well hidden from the travellers on the river. Before leaving, he reached into the pack for a scarf to tie around Julianna's mouth.

"Now just stay here till I git Katu. She will need some female company, someone to tell her that I am not to be trifled with."

Crump checked his money belt, lifted the pack of supplies from the dug-out and headed up the trail to Lousetown.

Julianna waited until Crump disappeared and then tried to wiggle out of the ropes. It was hot. She had not eaten since Fort Selkirk and had had little sleep in the past ten days. As she fought with the ropes, she felt faint. Her reserves were gone, and the ropes were too much for her. Julianna slumped against the tree and eventually fell into a fitful sleep.

She woke at the unpleasant sound of his voice. "Here's my beauty," Crump boasted.

Julianna opened her eyes to find herself face to face with the woman who had driven them on their journey over the past weeks. Katu was very slight, with dazzling dark eyes and smooth black hair that fell below her shoulders. She was the most beautiful person Julianna had ever seen.

Julianna smiled. "I'm called River Woman, and I've heard all about you from Salkusta."

"Salkusta will come and sink a knife into this dirty white man. I glad you are here, River Woman. Maybe we can look after each other." Katu was not the weak woman that Julianna had imagined from listening to Salkusta's stories of her.

When Crump was busy arranging the boat, Katu whispered to Julianna, "And maybe the two of us can look after him."

Crump returned to untie Julianna and take them to the dug-out.

"Now I will have a rest, and you girls will paddle me to Fort Yukon," he ordered. "Git in the front, Katu. We'll be in American territory by tomorrow night as long as you girls paddle hard. If you fool around, we will camp on the shore."

The girls paddled downriver at a good pace. Julianna and Katu were afraid of camping onshore with this despicable man. In the wilderness there would be no one to come to their rescue. Crump made them take the boat far out on the river so they could not call for help from the people crowded on the shores of the bustling new town.

Soon they passed the gold rush city and approached the Indian village of Moosehide. Again, Crump insisted on keeping a wide berth from this settlement and threatened to kill them if they called for help. Katu watched despondently as they passed her village.

Julianna dreaded to think of what lay ahead for her and Katu. They had a day's paddle before they would reach the American border. Once they were out of Canadian territory, there would be little hope of rescue, especially now that Salkusta and Split the Waves were in custody. Split the Waves had told Julianna stories of the American river settlements where the miners made the laws, and there was only rough justice. As long as Crump married Katu, no one would pay any attention to the fact that the native girl was forced into the arrangement. Without the protection of a family, Julianna would be considered easy prey for lawless men and would be treated with contempt because she was Katu's friend. If they ended up in Fort Yukon, all would be lost.

If they didn't escape now, they were doomed. "It is now or never," Julianna murmured to herself.

Suddenly, Julianna leaned all her weight on one side of the boat, and over they went. Katu, Crump and Julianna landed in the water. Crump tried to reach the boat but was swept downstream, cursing at the girls. His head bobbed up for a breath as he fought to stay afloat.

Julianna was ready for the swim and immediately looked around for Katu. The native girl was struggling in the water, trying to grab the boat. Julianna swam over to her companion and tried to hold her head above the water. Katu struggled frantically and would not let Julianna help her.

Julianna had always been able to self-rescue in any type of current and had been taught life saving, but this was her first real attempt at an actual rescue. Julianna remembered her life-saving lessons. *Calm the victim. Tell her to relax. Place your hand on the victim's chin and pull the victim to safety.* That was okay if you were in a swimming pool, but here they were in the cold waters of the Yukon River. Julianna grabbed Katu firmly under the chin.

"Don't fight me!" Julianna yelled. "Pretend to sleep on your back."

Finally Katu calmed down. The small woman rested on her back and let Julianna pull her to shore. They held each other up as they struggled out of the shallow water and fell onto the beach.

"Are you okay, Katu?" Julianna asked after she had caught her breath.

"We're saved! You are true to your name, River Woman," Katu smiled and hugged Julianna. The two young women burst into tears of relief and joy. They giggled, then danced on the sandy shoreline, and then hugged each other again.

They looked downstream to see if Crump had survived, but only the dug-out was in sight, drifting slowly into an eddy on the river's edge.

"He is so evil," Julianna remarked, "his body will pollute the river."

"At least he is out of our lives. Come now, River Woman, we go back to Moosehide. The Trondek people are there." Katu led Julianna along a trail that skirted the river. "My auntie will be there to care for us," Katu informed Julianna as they hiked along.

"But didn't your aunt and uncle sell you to Crump?" Julianna did not want Katu to be captured again.

"Not my auntie. It was her new husband, Harold, who has been crazed by drink. He kept me locked up, and my auntie did not know where I was. She pleaded with the new chief to rescue me, but he said it was a family matter and wouldn't interfere. My auntie left Harold and convinced the chief to have him banished from our tribe. Now she stays here in Moosehide."

They walked up the bank to a picturesque village built along the river. To Julianna, it seemed as if she had arrived in paradise. Here there would be food and dry clothes and a place to sleep. *If only Split the Waves and Salkusta were free.*

"Oh, darn it! All my clothes are in the dug-out, even my beautiful ceremonial dress. I'll have to wear these rags and everyone will think I'm poor."

"They will see you as an important woman, not for what you wear," Katu promised, "but for who you are. All the same, it doesn't hurt for a woman to look her best, so I will see that you are provided with suitable clothes. What did you say about a dress?"

"Jenny from the Tlingit people made me a beautiful dress of caribou skins. It is decorated with pink beads and beautiful shells. It was given to me for my ceremony when I became a woman." Julianna was still proud of how she had persisted with her training, learning the intricate stitches from the old grandmother.

"At my ceremony, I met Salkusta for the first time. That was when my father still lived and was chief. He would not let me marry Salkusta because I was expected to find a rich man for a husband, and Salkusta did not have blankets and guns. If only my father knew that I would be sold to that wicked, disgusting swindler he would regret not giving me to Salkusta."

"So is that why Salkusta became a trader?" Julianna asked. "Was he trying to earn enough money to buy you?"

"No, we are not bought," Katu protested. "Parents make sure that the husband is able to look after their daughter. A good husband has to hunt successfully for caribou and moose, and he should have blankets to give out at the wedding and supplies to give to the parents. That is the custom. Salkusta comes from a good family, but he had not earned the right to be married. Now I hear from the travellers that he is coming back with lots of gold and supplies."

"Oh no! The supplies!" Julianna cried. "Everything is in the boat. It will be lost."

"I don't think you will lose anything. My people will find the boat and bring it back to the village. No one takes another person's belongings here." Then, switching to a more interesting topic, Katu asked, "Is Split the Waves going to ask for you to be his wife?"

"No, I'm not getting married. I'm still searching for my family and hope to find out about them in Dawson," Julianna replied. "You see, I have forgotten who I am so Split the Waves' aunt adopted me into their family. Although I am proud to be River Woman of the Tlingits, I still yearn to find my own people."

"There's my auntie's house," Katu said. She called to her aunt and was greeted with hugs and tears. They were brought into the cabin and given hot, fresh bannock and a rich salmon stew. Julianna wanted to gobble down the food but remembered the lessons taught by the old grandmother and ate slowly, often thanking her hostess for the food. Before she had finished the meal, Julianna's eyes began to droop. She was afraid of being rude and would not tell Katu that she had not slept for days. She did not have to say anything to Katu's aunt.

"Come, you tired little bird," the aunt said kindly. "I can see you are about to fall asleep in your bowl."

She lead Julianna over to a cot and covered the exhausted girl with a wool blanket. It was cool and quiet in the cabin, and Julianna fell asleep before her head hit the pillow.

CHAPTER 14

MOOSEHIDE VILLAGE

While Julianna slept, her friends, accompanied by the Mounties, Gaston, the Kid, Joe and Anna, docked their boat outside of Lousetown.

"Turn in before the Trondek River. There is a trail leading to the village where we should find him," Salkusta instructed. To himself, he prayed that Katu would be safe. Split the Waves said little, but he feared the worst, believing his English friend was dead and that he had failed her.

The two policemen, Split the Waves and Salkusta made their way into Lousetown while Gaston and the Kid remained behind with Joe and his wife. Tents were scattered on every available spot of ground and the village was crowded with Klondikers. Only a few native people were seen among the crush of newcomers. Salkusta lead them to an Indian fishing site near the Klondike River.

"This fishing spot once belonged to Katu's father, but now it has fallen into Harold's hands. Instead of fishing, he is always drinking. The family is being destroyed by him," Salkusta explained sadly.

And it seemed as if destruction had occurred. The small cabin was littered with liquor bottles, and a drunken man lay on a cot.

Salkusta was the first into the cabin. "Where is she? Where is Katu? If you sold her to that piece of filth, I will beat you!"

But Salkusta already knew the truth for there was the pack of supplies stolen from Fort Selkirk, and on the table was the belt previously worn by Crump, only now part of the five thousand dollars had already been wasted on liquor.

"You sold her. She's gone with him!" Salkusta lunged at the sick man.

"Hold it, Salkusta," McKenzie cautioned. "That won't solve anything. It hasn't been long since Crump left. They can't have gone far. I'll take the pack with the supplies and the money belt. That will prove your innocence, and there will be no trial. You are free to go but if you want, you can come with Constable Winters and me. We will help you find the girls and chase down this villain."

Split the Waves did not even bother to ask the drunk about River Woman. Instead, he turned his thoughts to following Crump, hoping that his dear friend still lived.

"We want your help," Split the Waves replied. "Salkusta, these guys don't all hate the Indians. Remember when I told Kretch there were some good white guys."

Salkusta had difficulty remembering back to that carefree time when they were starting off on their trading trip, confident in themselves, and when he was happy to be on a trip that would lead him to Katu. Now Kretch was dead, and Katu and Julianna were in the hands of the most vile man in the Klondike.

The men rejoined the rest of their group back at the boat, and prepared to launch again. The Mounties, Gaston, the Kid, Split the Waves and Salkusta each took a paddle. Soon the craft was speeding to Dawson almost as fast as the great ocean-going boat of the Tlingits. They landed among a crush of boats on the Dawson waterfront. They searched among the thousands of boats but saw no sign of Crump or the dug-out. Gaston and the Kid agreed to take Joe and Anna to the hospital. The Mounties and the two young men continued the chase.

They left behind the bustling new City of Dawson and were approaching the Han village of Moosehide. Salkusta thought of how relieved he would be if only Katu could still be living with her people in the remote village. Katu's father had been chief, and although her mother had died many years ago, the young girl was dearly loved and cared for by family up until the time that Katu's aunt remarried.

Salkusta remembered back to the first time he met Katu. At her potlatch, Katu was clothed in the traditional dress, but this was a dress with a difference. Her aunt had spent months sewing the garment. The white hide was as soft as silk, adorned by thousands of pink beaded roses. That day, Katu walked into the potlatch house, her head lowered demurely. As she passed Salkusta, she smiled briefly at him and from that moment, Salkusta was hopelessly in love.

Her high-ranking family liked him, but Katu's father believed that a year apart would prove if the couple truly cared for one another. The chief encouraged Salkusta to seek his fortune and then return to ask for Katu's hand.

Everything had changed since his departure. Katu's father had died suddenly and Katu's aunt had married a drunkard. Salkusta swore under his breath that if only Katu could be saved, he would never touch drink and he would work hard every day of his life to look after his family. Salkusta's thoughts were interrupted by Split the Waves.

"Our dug-out. Look! See, it's caught in the willows."

They steered to shore and pulled the big trading boat upriver to a landing spot.

"What do you think, Salkusta?" Split the Waves asked.

"Everything in the boat is wet. They must have tipped!" Salkusta answered. Then the full impact of this hit him. "She don't swim," he cried. "She's drowned." Salkusta could not contain his emotions any longer. He kneeled on the bank and wailed in sorrow.

The Mounties encouraged Salkusta to have faith. The officers led the way along the trail into the village. Salkusta and Split the Waves directed the officers to the house of Katu's aunt, knowing that this was where they would learn the fate of their loved ones and of the criminal the Mounties were after.

As they approached the cabin, the door flew open, and Katu ran into Salkusta's arms. Now the young man cried again, but this time for joy. Split the Waves ran into the cabin, his heart pounding, believing River Woman had not survived but afraid to ask Katu lest the answer be the worst words he would ever hear. It was dark in the little cabin, making it difficult for him to see after being in the bright sunshine. He closed his eyes for a moment. When he had adjusted to the dim light, there on the cot he saw River Woman, sleeping peacefully.

"Hey, River Woman, wake up." He kissed her cheek. Julianna woke and threw her arms around Split the Waves.

"You're safe. They didn't kill you when you ran away? Are the police chasing you?"

Just then the two policemen walked in the door.

"You can't take him!" Julianna yelled. "He's innocent!"

McKenzie and Winters laughed, "Now don't you fret, Miss. We know Split the Waves is a good man and not a thief. We were helping Split the Waves and Salkusta find you and Katu and it looks like that part of our job is done. Now, we have to catch Crump and put him behind bars."

Julianna explained that Crump was last seen bobbing in the water and sinking out of sight, and added, "I guess your job is over after all."

"Not quite," Salkusta added. "You must come to our wedding, that is, if Katu's aunt will bless our marriage."

The aunt looked on with a relieved smile. "She's yours, and I do not want any dowry for her. I am deeply sorry that Harold caused all this grief, and I regret I didn't stop him from his evil ways. Now I get busy to make the wedding and the potlatch."

"I'll pay for the potlatch," Split the Waves said. "I will sell my trading supplies and have plenty of money for the potlatch and still more. River Woman enjoys a potlatch because she belongs to the Tlingit Nation."

"That is true, but I still wish to find my family. Do you have any news about a family who lost their fourteen-year-old daughter?" Julianna asked the Mounties.

"Split the Waves already asked us," Constable McKenzie replied solemnly, "and we've heard nothing. We will ask all the new arrivals and let you know. Certainly, no one would want to lose a fine daughter like you."

"Thank you," Julianna replied sadly.

The policemen joined them for lunch before poling upstream to Dawson. They left with a promise to return for the ceremony.

News of the impending wedding spread throughout the gold rush town. This wedding would be a special event for the people of Dawson, who tended to turn the smallest occasion into a reason for a major celebration. The church people, the store keepers who traded with the Trondek, the rich gold discoverers—Skookum Jim, Tagish Charlie, Carmacks and his wife—the poor of the native community and the rich, all anxiously awaited the wedding.

The cheechakos—the newcomers to Dawson—did not know how they should dress or what gifts to purchase. They had to seek advice from the oldtimers and the leaders in the native community. The wedding was the talk of the new gold rush city.

But one person who heard about the wedding was filled with terror. Harold had taken five thousand dollars in exchange for Katu, and now Crump was without his prize. Harold knew of Crump's temper and lived in constant fear of revenge. The more fearful Harold became, the more he turned to drink. In his alcoholic stupor, he would cry about his wrongful deed. He missed his wife and his friends at Moosehide. Now he would never again be allowed to return to the village and never be permitted to attend a potlatch for a wedding or a funeral. Even his own death would not be marked by a gathering of his people. His anguish became deeper and deeper. He was fearful of being killed by Crump and he was in despair because he had mistreated his wife's niece and now was an outcast. Harold finished his last bottle of whiskey beside the river. Then he walked to his death in the icy, fast-flowing waters of the Klondike River.

News of the native man's death spread through the community, as did the sorry circumstances. People knew of Crump and blamed the swindler for the death of the native man. They spoke of the villainy that would have led to a young woman being ruined.

Now there was even more excitement about the impending marriage. "A Trondek princess was to be married," was the news in the street. And this was a town that enjoyed stories of fame, of riches, but more than anything, the Klondikers enjoyed stories of true love.

That summer they heard of Stander, the rich and handsome gold miner who pursued his love, Violet, and finally won her hand in marriage. They also laughed over the tale of Swiftwater Bill, who took several hundred thousand in nuggets from the gold fields. Gussie Lamore, the object of his love, entered a cafe on the arms of a rival and ordered eggs, the most expensive item on the menu. In order to thwart his rival, Swiftwater Bill bought every egg in town and had them fried and flipped out the window to the hungry dogs.

The favourite story told by the Klondikers was of Mabel Long, an eighteen-year-old woman whose parents insisted she marry a man twenty years her senior. Before she and her older husband launched their scow at Bennett City, they sold a passage to a young man named Roseberg. Once the scow was out on the lake, a fierce squall raged down on them, kicking up the waters and sending the craft onto the rocks. When Mabel was flung into the water, Roseberg jumped in after her and carried her to shore. There they declared their love to each other, and young Mabel sobbed her despair at being forced to marry a man she did not love. The two young people fled along the lake on foot with the husband in pursuit. They were not caught and, as in fictional romances, it turned out that Roseberg was heir to a Boston fortune. Mabel was able to divorce her husband and marry her true love. The story of Katu and Salkusta was equally romantic and was now on the lips of everyone who believed in true love.

For her trips into Dawson City, Julianna wore the dress Split the Waves had given her at Sheep Camp. Attired fashionably, she was able to visit the shops to purchase food and clothing for the wedding. One of her tasks was to assist Katu's family with outfits for the ceremony. This entailed several shopping trips upriver to Dawson. With gold in her purse, Julianna set out to purchase a dress for Katu's aunt and other items for the wedding.

The city was bursting at the seams. Steamers arrived on the docks unloading tons of supplies, from the basics to the exotic. Dawson was the biggest city on the west side of the North American continent. You could purchase a Parisian dress and fancy food fit for the table of a king.

Julianna was not just interested in shopping. Most importantly, she wanted to find her family. Her first stop of the day was the mining recorder's office. The officials listened to Julianna's story and carefully searched their records for a missing fourteen year old but found nothing. They suggested she visit the churches and the registrar's office. Julianna called in at each place, but with no success. No one had reported a missing girl.

Julianna tried to put aside her worries and enjoy the sights of the new city. She passed the saloons and saw the elegant Regina Hotel with its floors covered with carpets from Brussels and its banisters trimmed with gold leaves. She saw a second hotel, the Fairview, which was even more elegant. After weeks in the bush and on the river, Julianna was fascinated by the buildings and the extravagance of the gold rush city.

She looked in the windows of the exclusive women's apparel shops, but when she checked the prices she knew she had to find the type of establishment that would cater to the more modest tastes of her new friends. Everything seemed so extreme, nothing appropriate for Katu's aunt. Julianna was looking in a store window when she felt a light tap on her shoulder and heard a pleasant, familiar voice say, "It's my guardian angel."

"Mrs. Hannah. You made it safely! Good for you. And how is John?"

"John is more than well. We were able to save the title to the claim and already I have received an offer of three hundred thousand dollars from Big Alex. I am just trying to decide whether to keep the claim or sell out. It is not the richest in the Klondike but still produces enough to give me a good living."

"What luck for you!" Julianna exclaimed.

"Come. I'll buy you tea in the Fairview, and we will catch up on all the events since we parted."

"But it is so expensive, Mrs. Hannah, I can't accept."

"Posh, child. That is enough. Had it not been for you and your friends, I would be back in San Francisco in a home for the destitute."

Julianna complied, and they exchanged stories in the ornate dining room, sipping tea and eating cakes sent from Seattle.

"This place is owned by Belinda Mulroney," Mrs. Hannah told Julianna. "She is sharp of tongue but one of the most enterprising young woman I have ever encountered. She never lets the men get the best of her. She advised me to sell out and put my money into a business. I have always wanted to have a hardware store and a dress shop and I love to sew clothes. John is happy to stay in the Klondike so I just may settle here and operate a business that I am much better at than gold mining. Besides," she continued, "his father, Patrick Moore, was well loved by this community and there are many people in the town who have given me their word that John will be well cared for should anything happen to me."

"Was that your son-in-law's name, Moore?" Julianna asked.

"Yes, dear, he's buried on the hillside. John visits his grave every Sunday."

"It is so strange," Julianna said, "but that name is familiar." Julianna looked pensive for a minute. "Why, it's my mother's maiden name! I can't be sure, because I can't even remember my own name."

"I know you will find your family again. Trust in Split the Waves. He is the one that will help you. He is very special," Mrs. Hannah advised. "Now you and I should go shopping. I can help you find just the right store to buy the dress for Katu's aunt."

"And you must buy a dress as well, for we want you at the ceremony, along with John," Julianna added happily.

The day of the wedding dawned sunny and warm. Salkusta waited in the small log church. He was dressed in a black suit, with a white shirt and black tie. The bishop smiled at Salkusta and told him to be patient, that his bride was worth waiting for. Split the Waves stood by the groom's side, also clothed in a dark formal suit.

The church was packed with people of both cultures. The wealthy with their expensive European clothing and gold nugget chains sat alongside the trappers and fishermen dressed in their beautifully sewn traditional garments. Gaston and the Kid had cleaned up and dressed in their finest for the celebration. Mrs. Hannah came with her grandson. Even Anna was able to accompany her husband, now that she had recovered from the worst of the scurvy attack and had left behind her irrational fear of river travel. It was an event the guests would talk about for years to come.

There was an appreciative murmur throughout the congregation as Katu and Julianna walked slowly down the isle. Katu was beautiful. Instead of the traditional native dress, she wore a full-length white gown that emphasized her narrow waist and billowed out in layers of crinoline and satin. A small veil crowned her dark head. Katu approached the altar with her head lowered. Julianna followed behind, dressed in her traditional native garment.

The Anglican bishop wore his bright, flowing robes, the choir sang and Katu's aunt cried when Salkusta and Katu were pronounced man and wife. When Salkusta finally took his bride in his arms, Julianna smiled at Split the Waves and blew him a kiss. At that moment, Julianna wished she could be content to remain with these people who loved her. Then, as she walked from the church, her memory returned for a minute and she could visualize the face of the boy she knew she loved, someone who was waiting for her to return.

Salkusta was a happy man that day. He was relieved to flee the church where he had been nervous and he was delighted at the extravagant potlatch that Split the Waves had arranged. It was not only Split the Waves who had worked to make the occasion so special. The Trondek people belonged to one of two clans, Wolf or Crow. To belong to a clan is like being a member of a very large family. It was the custom for the members of the Wolf clan to donate and prepare the food for Katu, who was of the Crow clan.

The celebration took place on the lawn beside the church where tables were decorated with wildflowers and laden with baked salmon, caribou stew, fresh vegetables, bannock, bread, cakes and fruit. Salkusta and his bride sat at the head table with Split the Waves and Julianna along with close members of Katu's family.

The Trondek chief used the occasion to make a long speech. He began by paying a tribute to Katu's father, the former chief, and to Katu's mother, who had been laid to rest many years before. He told the newcomers about his people—how this was the land of the Trondek, that they took their name from the river which the white people called Klondike.

"In white man's language, it means pounding, because at this site, my people pound sticks into the river bed to make fish weirs," the chief explained.

The chief continued to speak, recalling past events and great leaders. Some of the guests listened with interest, while others hoped the speech would soon end and the dancing begin. As the chief droned on, there was a gasp from the back of the gathering. A few people at the edge of the crowd turned to look as a wild-looking man approached. The swarthy man was bedraggled and staggered under the influence of liquor. *Surely this was not a guest coming late to the wedding?*

"She's mine," he yelled pulling a pistol from beneath his vest.

People cried out in terror and ducked under the tables or ran from their seats. Salkusta threw himself in front of Katu.

"You took my money," Crump screamed, "now I demand you hand over my woman."

"Here's your money!" Salkusta yelled. He opened the gold poke Split the Waves had given him to pay Crump and threw the nuggets at the evil man. The gold scattered across the tables and onto the grass.

Crump dropped the pistol and ran through the crowd, picking up a nugget here and one there, then he crawled on the ground seeking the small gold pieces. Constables Winters and McKenzie moved slowly towards the villain, while other guests scattered away from this frightening man. As the crazed man tried to retrieve the nuggets scattered about, he puffed and gasped. Then, as Crump grabbed for a nugget beyond his reach, he gave out a moan, clutched his chest and collapsed.

McKenzie and Winters were the first to reach the stricken man. The villain's heart had given out, and Crump was pronounced dead.

"He lived a vile life," the chief said, "and died of the greed that has taken over his soul. He is a warning to all of us that we must live our lives, not for the selfish causes, but for the good of our families and our neighbours. Don't let this event mar the festivities. It is a sign to all of us."

The crowd agreed. The Mounties laid Crump in the boat so he could be transported later to the coroner. Soon the fiddlers started up, and the dancing began.

CHAPTER 15

THE JOURNEY HOME

After the wedding, Split the Waves busied himself selling the remaining goods he had transported from Klukwan. He kept several packs to bring back to his village on the Alsek where his grandmother waited. Split the Waves was anxious to bring her the blankets he had promised. More than that, he knew she believed he had died in the flood and he wanted to relieve the pain she must be suffering.

Split the Waves thought that Julianna might want to stay in Moosehide. Katu's family accepted Julianna as a high-ranking Tlingit. When the village learned that Julianna might remain at Moosehide, there was considerable excitement. Several mothers hoped Julianna would choose their son as a husband. When Julianna and Katu walked through the village one afternoon, an Elder took Julianna by the hand and brought her over to a line of young men.

Julianna could not understand what the old woman was saying and turned to Katu.

"She says that if you are not going to marry Split the Waves you should chose one of the men from Moosehide," Katu said with a twinkle in her eyes.

Julianna's face turned red. She did not want to be rude to the people who had taken her in. Although she cared for Split the Waves, she was not prepared to marry him. If she did not marry Split the Waves, she would marry no one.

"What shall I say?" Julianna asked. "I don't want to hurt their feelings."

"Tell them what is in your heart," Katu answered. "That is always the best when you are with our people. The young men understand your language."

"Thank you for your kind offer. I like your people, and I love Moosehide. However, I cannot marry yet. I have lost my memory and do not recall who I am or where I come from. I have to travel with Split the Waves. He found me after I lost my people, and he will be the one who can help me find my way home."

Katu translated this speech to the Elder who nodded her head and then took Julianna's hand in hers. In the Han language she told Julianna that she must go and find where her heart belonged.

When Split the Waves returned from a trading trip in Dawson, Julianna met him at the riverbank.

"I want to go with you to the Alsek. Can you help me get back to my people?"

"If you are brave enough, you will find them and I will go with you as far as I can. The steamer *Flora* goes upriver tomorrow. Can you be ready to go?"

"I am ready now, but it would be good to have another day with Katu and Salkusta."

It was sad for Julianna to leave her friends, especially Salkusta who had shared hardships and laughter with her. She was pleased at the happiness he had found.

"Hey, you know that Mrs. Hannah has given us jobs in her store," Salkusta announced. "I sell the hardware, cut wood, get meat for everyone, and Katu will sew beautiful dresses. Someday, we will have our own store, and we will live well," Salkusta said proudly.

Salkusta and Katu came to see them off at the dock in Dawson. Katu and Julianna hugged each other.

"You are my sister," Katu said, "and you are always welcome in my village."

Julianna had tears in her eyes as the little steamer pulled out into the river, heading upstream towards Whitehorse.

This journey was the easiest Julianna had made since Split the Waves had found her on the banks of the Alsek. Now they each had a berth with a clean cot, and there was a dining room that served hearty meals. Split the Waves and Julianna had nothing to do but sit on the deck and watch the beautiful hills slip by.

However, there were two passengers who were not so pleased with the accommodations. Mrs. Hitchcock, the widow of an American admiral, and Miss Van Buren, niece of an American president, were the first tourists to travel to Dawson City. The wealthy women arrived in the frontier town with the most amazing conglomeration of supplies. Their trunks and boxes transferred up to the Klondike included an ice cream freezer, two cages of live pigeons, a portable bowling alley, two great Danes, an enormous marquee to entertain in, and containers of rare food.

While in Dawson, these American women singled out the rich and famous and invited them to dinners. Now, the two portly women were travelling back to Whitehorse in the cramped boat. What was luxury for Julianna and Split the Waves was unacceptable to Mrs. Hitchcock and Miss Van Buren. Their shrill voices resounded throughout the little ship. They were outraged by the size of their cabins. They complained that there was no running water and that the food was atrocious.

Split the Waves and Julianna listened to this uproar with amusement.

"If that is the way the rich behave," Julianna said with a chuckle, "I just want to be ordinary."

"There are many millionaires in Dawson who do not change, despite their wealth. They have several million in gold, yet continue to work their claims and live in shacks. They spend money when they go outside to San Francisco but never let their wealth destroy their friendships. Take Skookum Jim. He will always remain part of the people from Caribou Crossing."

"Are you going to be wealthy and marry into a high-ranking family?" Julianna asked.

Split the Waves was somber and said nothing for a few minutes. "I guess you know that I would marry you if you wished, but I know that you still long to find your family and will not be content with me. Am I right?"

"There were times when all I wanted was to live my life with you and your people. Recently, I've had flashes from my past and know I must return to my people. But, I am not going back the same person. I've left behind the girl who could not talk to a young man without poison on my tongue. Now I feel good about myself," Julianna responded.

"Then we shall return to the place where you lost them. I had a dream that they wait for you in the canyon. That is where I take you. I hope that you will find them, but I fear that I will lose you."

Their serious conversation was broken by the shrill voices of the two New York women who couldn't bring themselves to wash in water dipped up from the Yukon River.

In a few days, the steamer reached the mouth of the Takhini River where it stopped for wood and where Julianna and Split the Waves disembarked. They were able to catch a ride with a Ta'an family for the trip upstream to Mendenhall. Now they passed through a valley where caribou grazed on the hills so thick that the herd turned the hillside black. The river valley was unspoiled, with only bush and the occasional fishing camp along the sandy banks.

By evening, they reached Mendenhall and the beginning of the trail over to the headwaters of the Alsek River. Split the Waves was able to hire two young men to pack for them. They had a pleasant hike over the old trail. At Champagne they began their river journey that would take them to the Alsek River.

Split the Waves retrieved a boat he had left with friends and soon they were paddling down the winding Dezadeash River. As the valley opened up, the glacier-covered mountains created a spectacular backdrop above the river. The two friends enjoyed the warm sunshine and the beauty and peace of the country. They would soon reach the treacherous Alsek and neither of them wanted to dwell on what lay ahead for them.

Soon after the Dezadeash River flowed into the Alsek, they came upon Split the Waves' village. All but a few of the people had left to fish salmon in a nearby river. Split the Waves' grandmother had remained behind. She was sitting by the fire when they paddled to shore, and did not see them land. Split the Waves walked up the bank and called to her.

The old woman held out her arms to her grandson and cried.

Split the Waves and Julianna made tea for the grandmother and gave her a soft blanket, flour, sugar and fruit. They spent the night in the village and prepared to leave early in the morning. Again the grandmother begged Split the Waves to stay behind, telling him that it was time he married his woman and had children. Split the Waves told her with a smile that he was too old now to be bossed about.

Split the Waves brought out two small dug-outs and loaded them with furs to trade. Soon they were in the flat valley, paddling towards Turnback Canyon. There was no wind, and they were able to speed across the flats. They stopped in a quiet eddy before entering the canyon. They camped on the river's edge and talked long into the night. Both felt that this night might be their last evening together and wanted to share all their thoughts. As the night went on, memories of her earlier life flitted through Julianna's thoughts.

"I'm called...Julianna," she said. "I almost recall everything and then my memories are lost again."

"You are going home, my friend," Split the Waves said sadly.

Split the Waves took Julianna's hand and kissed her fingers. "And now I want to hold you one last time," he said. Split the Waves placed his arms around Julianna, softly kissed each cheek and then her lips. It was a long, lingering kiss, gentle and sweet. Julianna had never been kissed before. Tears fell down her cheeks when their lips parted. He brushed the tears away before releasing her from his arms.

"I will always be near you, through all the years of your life," Split the Waves told her. "Now we must go. We will go down the canyon with our boats side by side. I will be there to look after you. Now this may be frightening for you, but we must tip when we get to the ledge where you dented that funny hat you used to have. Can you do that if I give you my word I will not let harm come to you?"

"I trust you, Split the Waves, but please don't you take any risks. It is very dangerous."

"I've been down this canyon many times and look, I still breathe the air, laugh and eat. Give me your hand." He held her hand against his chest. "I promise you will find your way back to where your heart is. And now, it's time to go," Split the Waves said softly, his voice breaking.

They paddled the first part of the canyon without incident. The water was lower now and easier to navigate. They were side by side as they crossed the flat area before the ledge. Julianna's heart pounded, remembering the plunge into the hole.

Split the Waves drew up beside her. "I hope I am in that other life of yours," he said. "Good-bye for now, River Woman."

"I will always care for you," Julianna whispered.

They were at the ledge. They gave each other one last glance before their boats plunged into the fury of the canyon.

She could still feel the kiss when she woke. She coughed and drew in gasps of air. Strong loving arms held her close.

"Oh Graham," she murmured. "You're okay."

"I thought I lost you," Graham said, "but you came back to me. You've been unconscious for two days and then, just a minute ago, you stopped breathing and I thought you were dying."

"The others! Did everyone make it to safety?" Julianna thought of the Kid and Gaston, no, Mr. Robertson and Charles.

"They are all safe. First, I will get you some tea, then we will tell you everything."

The rest of the group were sitting about the fire. There were cries of joy when they heard that Julianna was well. Ms. Lindsay was the first into the tent to check on her student.

"Julianna," Ms. Lindsay said smiling, "I can't tell you how relieved I am. We will get you back to Whitehorse today and into the hospital."

"What about Dietmar? Did he survive?"

"Not only did he survive but he rescued you and Graham. He paddled down to the coast to call in a helicopter. We expect to be out of here soon."

"I want to get up," Julianna said. "Can you help me?"

Ms. Lindsay and Graham helped Julianna to the fire.

"Tell me about the rescue," Julianna asked. "What happened after we went over? I can't remember a thing."

"Graham never let go of you," Ms. Lindsay explained, "even though he must have been thrashed about like a matchstick. Dietmar was close by. Graham grabbed the end of the kayak and Dietmar dragged you both to shore."

"I was afraid you were dead," Graham interjected, "but you were only unconscious. I could see where your helmet had smashed into the canyon wall so hard it dented. See!" Graham held it up for Julianna's inspection.

"Mr. Robertson was able to get to shore and climb up on the bank just downriver from us," Graham continued. "I stayed with you and saw Charles swept down the river. At first we couldn't see him, but could hear him blow on that whistle of his. He managed to get into a small eddy where he clung to the side of the canyon. Charles was just about a goner."

"Mr. Robertson did not think twice about his own safety," Charles said. "He swam across the river and caught me when I knew I couldn't hold on for another second. By that time, Dietmar was able to get to me and pull me to safety and returned later to bring Mr. Robertson across."

"I guess I learned more on this trip than you students," Mr. Robertson said contritely.

"And what about you and the others, Ms. Lindsay?" Julianna asked.

"We had no idea of the accident. We were hiking across the glacier and arrived to find an encampment of frightened, exhausted rafters, all worried about you, Julianna."

They heard the helicopter approach from down the valley. It landed on a level spot marked by flagging tape. Dietmar jumped out the door, rushed over to Julianna and gave her a brotherly hug. Not only was Dietmar delighted at Julianna's recovery, he also had good news about a job guiding on the river.

"So you will not have to return to the polluted European city," Ms. Lindsay remarked.

"And you will not wander all the days of your life and then die before you find your true love, like in your song," Julianna added. "And thank you for rescuing Graham and me."

Julianna and Graham sat together at the back of the helicopter. As they flew back to Whitehorse, Graham took her hand and drew it up to his lips.

"I never want to leave you again," Graham said. "It frightened me so much when I thought you would die."

"I've missed you too," Julianna admitted, "but I believe you were with me all the time. I had such a strange dream about a journey with a boy who looked like you. All I wanted was to come back to my family and be your friend again."

Julianna tried to remember the trip over the pass, the race to the Klondike, and the young man who reminded her so much of Graham. But already the memory of Split the Waves, Salkusta and Katu was blending into the present. Although the memories would fade, her remarkable journey would be with her always, guiding Julianna throughout her life.

ABOUT THE AUTHOR

Yvonne Harris is an avid canoeist whose journeys down the Yukon and Alaskan rivers form the backdrop for her young adult and children's adventure stories. Her earlier books are *River Fairies*, *The Caves of Chlingitani* and *Gwitchin Quest*.

ABOUT THE ILLUSTRATOR

Yukon artist Catherine Deer has spent her life in the North, making Whitehorse her home since 1969. Often focusing on the Yukon's wildlife, places and people for her subject matter, Catherine has also illustrated a number of young people's books, previous to the cover of *Back to the Klondike*. Catherine lives with her husband Eric and two sons Tyler and Anders.